FRO
NANCY DREW

THE CASE: *Crime is in fashion, and Nancy's looking to catch the rip-off artist in the act.*

CONTACT: *Bess is about to make her modeling debut . . . unless the shoplifter steals the show.*

SUSPECTS: Lesley Richards—*For a mall rat who loves to shop, stealing may be the only way to pay off her credit card bills.*

Craig Jordan—*A maintenance worker at the mall, he may have found a way to clean up financially as well.*

Mara Morrell—*She designed the jackets and now may have come up with the perfect way to publicize them: grand larceny.*

COMPLICATIONS: *Nancy knows that someone in this case is bound to get hurt . . . and it could be Bess. Nancy's friend loves to wear trendy clothes, but she also wears her heart on her sleeve.*

Books in The Nancy Drew Files™ Series

#1 SECRETS CAN KILL
#2 DEADLY INTENT
#3 MURDER ON ICE
#4 SMILE AND SAY MURDER
#5 HIT AND RUN HOLIDAY
#6 WHITE WATER TERROR
#7 DEADLY DOUBLES
#8 TWO POINTS TO MURDER
#9 FALSE MOVES
#10 BURIED SECRETS
#11 HEART OF DANGER
#16 NEVER SAY DIE
#17 STAY TUNED FOR DANGER
#19 SISTERS IN CRIME
#31 TROUBLE IN TAHITI
#35 BAD MEDICINE
#36 OVER THE EDGE
#37 LAST DANCE
#41 SOMETHING TO HIDE
#43 FALSE IMPRESSIONS
#45 OUT OF BOUNDS
#46 WIN, PLACE OR DIE
#49 PORTRAIT IN CRIME
#50 DEEP SECRETS
#51 A MODEL CRIME
#53 TRAIL OF LIES
#54 COLD AS ICE
#55 DON'T LOOK TWICE
#56 MAKE NO MISTAKE
#57 INTO THIN AIR
#58 HOT PURSUIT
#59 HIGH RISK
#60 POISON PEN
#61 SWEET REVENGE
#62 EASY MARKS
#63 MIXED SIGNALS
#64 THE WRONG TRACK
#65 FINAL NOTES
#66 TALL, DARK AND DEADLY
#68 CROSSCURRENTS
#70 CUTTING EDGE
#71 HOT TRACKS
#72 SWISS SECRETS
#73 RENDEZVOUS IN ROME
#74 GREEK ODYSSEY
#75 A TALENT FOR MURDER
#76 THE PERFECT PLOT
#77 DANGER ON PARADE
#78 UPDATE ON CRIME
#79 NO LAUGHING MATTER
#80 POWER OF SUGGESTION
#81 MAKING WAVES
#82 DANGEROUS RELATIONS
#83 DIAMOND DECEIT
#84 CHOOSING SIDES
#85 SEA OF SUSPICION
#86 LET'S TALK TERROR
#87 MOVING TARGET
#88 FALSE PRETENSES
#89 DESIGNS IN CRIME
#90 STAGE FRIGHT
#91 IF LOOKS COULD KILL
#92 MY DEADLY VALENTINE
#93 HOTLINE TO DANGER
#94 ILLUSIONS OF EVIL
#95 AN INSTINCT FOR TROUBLE
#96 THE RUNAWAY BRIDE
#97 SQUEEZE PLAY
#98 ISLAND OF SECRETS
#99 THE CHEATING HEART
#100 DANCE TILL YOU DIE
#101 THE PICTURE OF GUILT
#102 COUNTERFEIT CHRISTMAS
#103 HEART OF ICE
#104 KISS AND TELL
#105 STOLEN AFFECTIONS
#106 FLYING TOO HIGH
#107 ANYTHING FOR LOVE
#108 CAPTIVE HEART
#109 LOVE NOTES
#110 HIDDEN MEANINGS
#111 THE STOLEN KISS
#112 FOR LOVE OR MONEY
#113 WICKED WAYS

Available from ARCHWAY Paperbacks

WICKED WAYS

CAROLYN KEENE

AN ARCHWAY PAPERBACK
Published by POCKET BOOKS
New York London Toronto Sydney Tokyo Singapore

AN ARCHWAY PAPERBACK *Original*

An Archway Paperback published by
POCKET BOOKS, a division of Simon & Schuster Inc.
1230 Avenue of the Americas, New York, NY 10020

ISBN: 0-671-50353-7

First Archway Paperback printing February 1996

10 9 8 7 6 5 4 3

Printed in the U.S.A.

IL 6+

WICKED WAYS

Chapter One

"It's hopeless!" Bess Marvin cried, staring into the mirror. She pulled and tugged at the dark pageboy wig she was trying to position on her head. Finally, in frustration, she tore the wig off completely, letting her long blond hair tumble down around her face. "*I'm* hopeless!"

Standing beside Bess at the mirror, Nancy Drew smothered a smile and took a moment to straighten her own reddish blond ponytail. The girls were in the employees lounge at Wicked, a trendy boutique at the River Heights Mall where Bess had recently begun working. Like most of the other salesclerks at Wicked, Bess had been asked to model in designer Mara Morrell's fashion show, which was scheduled to start in an hour on a runway set up just outside the store. Bess was thrilled but very nervous, and Nancy and her other best friend, Bess's cousin George Fayne, had come along to lend Bess moral support.

That morning's show was the kickoff of the Midwest Regional Retail Association's Spring Fashion Week. River Heights's Chamber of Commerce had wooed the association's prestigious seasonal show to town. It was a coup for the local business community and a chance for a good time for the area's fashion-conscious teens.

Bess made a face at her reflection, then gazed longingly at the glossy publicity shot of pop star Lynxette that was taped to the glass. The dark-haired singer was clad all in black, except for her satiny, electric blue bomber jacket.

"Wig or no wig, I'll never look like Lynxette," Bess declared, and straightened the scoop neck of her fuzzy black sweater. She turned sideways in front of the mirror, tugged at her short flippy black skirt, and tried to pull her stomach in.

"Well, I think it's a crazy idea, to have all the models in the Mara Morrell fashion show dress as Lynxette look-alikes just to promote Mara's bomber jackets," George remarked, depositing her in-line skates under the dressing table. She picked up the wig and plunked it on top of her own short dark curls. Using a hairbrush as a microphone, George strutted across the small lounge. "Oooooo—babe!" she crooned in a gravelly voice. "I got a bad case of blue and a worse case of you."

Nancy and Bess burst into laughter. "Somehow I can't imagine Lynxette ever wearing sweats," Nancy said as she plucked the wig off George's head.

"Here," she went on, making Bess sit down in front of the mirror, "let me help. By the time I'm finished, you'll look more like Lynxette than Lynxette herself." It was only a little white lie, thought Nancy. Pretty, curvy Bess would never resemble the high-cheekboned, ultraskinny rock idol. But telling Bess that would only break her heart.

Nancy pulled a sheer stocking cap out of the makeup kit on the dressing table. Deftly, she twisted Bess's silky hair up into a knot and tucked it under the cap. "There," she said, as she slipped the wig on Bess's head and secured it with a couple of bobby pins, "you're as gorgeous as Lynxette."

"No way!" Bess scoffed, but blushed a little and peered more closely at her reflection in the mirror. "You know," she said, lifting her blue eyes to meet Nancy's, "I've always dreamed of modeling."

"Look out, world, here comes cover girl Bess Marvin," George teased.

Bess playfully whacked George's arm with her eyeliner pencil. Then she got up and took a satiny, tangerine-colored bomber jacket off a rack of show clothes and slipped it on. A big needlepoint patch of a vintage electric guitar covered the back. It was one of the famous Mara Morrell jackets, which Bess and the other Lynxette look-alikes would be modeling. Ever since Lynxette had worn one in her last video, the jackets had become the hottest fashion item of the season.

Mara Morrell herself would be unveiling a select group of her latest jackets today as part of her new spring line. Other fashion shows would be going on throughout the week, as well as dozens of special events and promotions. Nancy, Bess, and George had already planned to shop till they dropped during the week's big sales.

"So when is Lynxette going to be here?" George asked as she finished tying the laces on her high-tops.

"Is she really coming?" Nancy asked in surprise. "I thought that was just a rumor."

"Nope. It's for real," Bess said. "Dan knows someone in her entourage. He says it's definitely on for the end of the week."

"Could that be Dan, as in Dan Schaffer?"

Bess blushed as she grinned at Nancy. "Could be."

"When do we finally get to meet this Dan person?" George asked. "I'm dying to check him out."

Bess lifted her eyebrows. "We've only been dating for a week. I can't drag him around to meet everyone I know."

"You've made him sound *very* interesting," Nancy pointed out. "How come he's got the inside scoop on Lynxette's comings and goings?"

Bess shrugged. "Lots of kids who work in CD City are hooked into the music scene. A sales rep clued him in last week."

Just then two other salesclerks from Wicked came giggling and laughing into the lounge. They squeezed past Nancy to get to their lockers. Both were already dressed in Lynxette wigs and Morrell jackets.

Right behind them was a slender woman in her late twenties, dressed in a short-skirted gray suit and medium high pumps. Her short blond hair was swept back off her face, playing up her prominent cheekbones and large dark eyes. Nancy noticed she seemed almost as nervous as Bess.

"Hi, Ms. Long," Bess said, greeting her. Nancy realized this was the boutique manager.

Ms. Long flashed an edgy smile at Bess, then addressed all her sales staff. "Lisa, Susan, are you ready? Mara Morrell just called from her car phone. She'll be here in twenty minutes. She wants to start the show as soon as she arrives."

Lisa and Susan were all smiles, but Bess still looked nervous. "I'm ready—I think," she said.

Ms. Long looked at Bess and nodded. "You look great, Bess." Then she noticed Bess's high-heeled ankle boots. "Be careful on the runway with those heels," she said. "The platform is high, and they set it up right at the edge of the balcony. I wouldn't trust the temporary railing that maintenance put up. I'd hate to see you doing a swan dive into the fountain down in the central court."

"Don't worry, Ms. Long. I'll be careful."

"Good. Since you're all ready, you girls should go back into the store and help. Fashion week has brought in a pretty big crowd already. Good for business, of course, but even better for shoplifters. I don't want to lose any more Morrell jackets."

Nancy's ears perked up. "Shoplifting?" she repeated to Bess after Ms. Long left the room.

Bess nodded as they filed through the narrow hallway that led back to the sales floor. "Someone's been stealing Morrell jackets. Just this morning another one vanished—a white one with a black cat on the back. It's the third one we've lost, and the thieves have hit other stores in the mall. Today's Woman lost two, the Chic Boutique four." Bess dropped her voice. "I heard Ms. Long on the phone yesterday with security. These jackets have been targeted by shoplifters all over the state."

Nancy was puzzled as they stepped into the brightly lit store. It was jammed with shelves full of sweaters, slacks, jeans. One rack of filmy print dresses caught Nancy's eye, but the price tags made her heart sink. Wicked was an upscale boutique, beyond Nancy's usual budget—except at sale time. She questioned Bess. "Morrell jackets are fun, but they aren't that expensive, at least compared to a lot of Wicked's stock. Why wouldn't a shoplifter take something more valuable?"

George looked up from a rack of some leather jackets. "These are worth twice as much."

"Morrell jackets are already collector's items," Bess explained. "No two of Mara's jackets are alike. They come in fifteen colors, and each patch is used only once on each color. Ms. Long thinks the thieves are trying to snatch up as many jackets as they can, so they can sell them for a lot of money when they become scarce."

"Sort of like baseball cards?" George asked as she sidled past two circular racks of blouses.

"Right," Bess said. "It was the hard-core Lynxette fans who started the craze. In Lynxette's last video there must've been about fifty dancers wearing Morrell jackets."

"So those jackets are definitely collector's items now," Nancy figured aloud.

"Yes, and guess what?" Bess said, clearly excited. "Dan told me that Lynxette is planning to shoot her next video right here at the mall as the grand finale of Fashion Week. The whole plan's been under wraps until today—Mara Morrell is supposed to announce it after the second half of her show this afternoon." Bess smoothed the tangerine jacket she was wearing. "Dozens of girls in the new video will wear Morrell jackets."

"That should inspire the shoplifters," said Nancy. "Too bad. A crime spree will put a damper on the fun of watching the video shoot."

Nancy scrutinized the store. Security cameras were discreetly placed in all the right spots: above the shelves behind the cash register, and in the corners with a good view of the door. "I imagine security will be beefed up for the occasion."

"It already has been," Bess confided, sounding worried again. "We've just finished installing a new state-of-the-art security system, like a lot of the smaller stores in the mall. But it hasn't stopped the thief or thieves so far."

Nancy thumbed through some jackets on a rack. None were chained together or secured to the rod with a lock. She felt the inside seams of one of the Morrell jackets, and quickly found what she was looking for. A plastic security tag, the kind that would set off alarms if the jackets were taken from the store before they were removed.

"How do these tags work?" Nancy asked Bess.

"I'm not sure exactly," Bess said, toying with her bracelet. "We have a handheld device that deactivates and removes the tag when customers pay at the register. Actually," Bess added, "we have two of them, for when we get busy. Ms. Long chose that kind of system so the customers would feel free to try things on without having to get one of us to unlock them. It's supposed to be foolproof."

Obviously it wasn't, Nancy thought. "Does your jacket have a tag?"

"No," Bess said. "None of the clothes on

the rack in the lounge do, because they've already been picked for us to wear at the show. We don't want to set off alarms when we leave the store to model."

"I doubt that anyone's going to rip a jacket off a model's back," George added.

"True," Nancy agreed.

Bess looked uneasy. "But it will be a madhouse when Lynxette films that video at the end of the week. Just watch what happens today when Mara Morrell shows up. She's going to raffle off one of her jackets. All the Lynxette-heads will go nuts."

"Well, what I can't wait to watch is you coming down that runway," George commented. "Flashes going off—"

"Flashes?" Bess stopped dead in her tracks. "Nancy, where's your camera?"

"In the shop being fixed." At the horrified expression on Bess's face, Nancy quickly added, "Don't worry. George brought hers."

George pulled a yellow waterproof sports camera from her backpack.

Bess's face fell. "Isn't that what you use when you scuba dive? Does it even have a flash?"

"It's a great camera, Bess. Flash and all." George gave her cousin a quick squeeze. "And you know I'm a good photographer, so just calm down. We'll get plenty of good shots of you modeling."

"Hmmm?" Nancy had been distracted by a pair of chili-pepper red cowboy boots on display in Wicked's shoe section. They would look great with the slim black jeans she was wearing and a candy-apple red Morrell jacket, she thought.

"Now, Bess," Ms. Long said as she came out from behind the counter, "I'm going in back for a minute. Stay at the register, but watch for shoplifters. If anything else is taken, I may have to pull you girls from the show to keep a full staff here."

As Ms. Long walked away, Bess took Nancy's arm. "You don't think she's serious, do you?"

"Don't worry, Bess," Nancy tried to reassure her friend. "Nothing will happen. You keep an eye on things in here, and George and I will keep our eyes peeled outside."

"Great," Bess said, only slightly relieved. "But you guys won't forget to take pictures, will you?"

"We won't forget," Nancy said as she steered George out of the store. "See you after the show."

Just outside the store Nancy looked around. Wicked was on the second floor of the mall in the main strip of stores, just to the right of the escalators and the railing that overlooked the mall atrium below. The runway and modeling platform had been set up only yards from the trendy boutique. Workers were on tall portable scaffolds, adjusting spotlights and focusing them on the runway.

Nancy and George made their way past a

curtained area at the end of the runway and peered over the balcony railing. A higher temporary railing had been set up along the outside edge of the runway to keep the models from falling from the narrow platform. Nancy looked down at the spouting fountain in the middle of a large shallow pool in the mall's central court. It was a long way down, she thought.

George pointed toward CD City, just below. "That's where Dan works. Maybe we should check it out, see if we can guess which guy is Bess's type."

Nancy chuckled. "Bess loves all types, George."

"I wonder if Dan's coming to see Bess in the show," George said as they walked toward the escalator. A small crowd had gathered in front of the runway, waiting while mall personnel in khaki shirts finished setting up chairs.

"From what Bess has said about him I'm sure he wouldn't miss it—" Nancy said, then realized George wasn't paying any attention.

Nancy followed the direction of George's gaze and raised her eyebrows. George's dark eyes were riveted on a cute square-jawed guy in a long, tweed overcoat. He was tall, the kind of guy George always preferred. A serious expression crossed his face as he looked past Nancy and George toward Wicked. Nancy could feel the intensity of his gaze from where she stood. She could see why he had caught George's eye.

Nancy elbowed George. "So why don't you go over and say hi?"

"To who?" George said, then colored slightly and laughed. "But I don't know him."

"Introduce yourself," Nancy urged. She noticed him head off toward Blazes, the in-line skating store. "Maybe he shares your passion for skating. RinkWorld has a skate dance later."

"Not so fast—but I'll check him out. If Mr. X isn't friendly, I'll just pick up new brakes for my skates. Meet you back here for the show."

With that, George hitched up the shoulder of her boatneck sweatshirt over her teal blue tank top and headed toward the in-line skating store.

Nancy watched Mr. X bypass Blazes and disappear around a corner. With a wink over her shoulder at Nancy, George casually followed behind.

Nancy turned back to watch the fashion show preparations, smiling at the thought of George's new interest. But a moment later her expression changed to one of shock, as an alarm blared across the mall.

Before Nancy could locate the source of the alarm she heard a familiar voice, screaming.

"Help!"

Nancy gasped. Bess was racing out of Wicked toward the runway, her tangerine jacket flapping. "Help!" she screamed again.

Chapter Two

NANCY DASHED toward the store. Had the thief struck again?

"Bess, what happened?"

"Thank goodness you're here. We need help fast." Bess pointed a shaky finger toward the rear of the boutique, then looked past Nancy's shoulder. "Where's security?" she wailed.

Nancy ran in, sidestepping all the bewildered customers. She noticed that no one was watching the cash register. "Bess," she yelled over her shoulder, "the register!" When she reached the back of the store, Nancy pushed through the door marked Employees Only. At the end of the hall past the employees' lounge, she saw four saleswomen, all in their dark Lynxette wigs, clustered around the door to the manager's small office.

"Ms. Long's locked in," one of the girls cried, over the continuing screech of the alarm.

From inside the office the store manager yelled. "Open up! Let me out!" Her shouts were punctuated by loud pounding on the door.

A guy in jeans and a black T-shirt was kneeling in front of the door, a red toolbox by his side.

Nancy pushed past the sales staff and saw that a nail had been crudely jammed into the lock. The guy was trying to pry it out with a screwdriver.

"It won't budge," he said, pushing his sandy brown hair out of his face. At the sight of Nancy he furrowed his brow slightly.

Nancy knelt down beside him and pulled some pliers from the tool kit. "Try these," she suggested.

"What's happening out there?" Ms. Long yelled.

"We'll have you out in just a second," Nancy called back.

"Please—hurry! And someone check the store up front." Ms. Long ordered.

"Kris is up front, back from her break," Bess yelled. She wedged her way into the crowded space and urged on the guy with the toolbox. "Hurry, Dan," she said softly. "Ms. Long sounds like she's about to lose it." Bess put her hand on his shoulder, and Nancy realized the compact, muscular guy must be Bess's new boyfriend.

"Hang on. I think I can get it." The guy bit his bottom lip as he worked the screwdriver into the keyhole and pulled the nailhead with the pliers. "There!" he said, and opened the door.

Ms. Long burst out, breathing hard. "Call security" were her first words. Nancy instinctively took the woman's arm to steady her. Ms. Long's face was sweaty from struggling with the door, and her suit was rumpled.

"I called them already," Bess said quickly. "But they haven't come yet or even killed the alarm."

"What set it off?" Nancy asked as one of the employees brought Ms. Long some water.

"I did," the manager replied. "I have a panic button in my office. Security should be here by now." She stopped to sip some water and went on. "Who locked me in there?"

"We don't know," Bess said. "We heard the alarm, then we heard you shouting. Right, Lisa?" She turned to the girl next to her, who was at least as tall as George and thin as a rail.

"That's right, Ms. Long. I was the first one here. I tried to open the door, but the lock was jammed. It's a lucky thing Dan was here and found the toolbox."

Nancy watched as Dan made his way toward the fire exit at the end of the hall. He reached up to a metal electrical box in a corner and switched off one of the circuit breakers. The alarm, which had been jangling nonstop, suddenly went off. Nancy wrinkled her brow, surprised that Dan knew where it was. Then she remembered he also worked at a store in the mall and was probably familiar with the security layout.

"Lisa!" Ms. Long suddenly gasped. "Where's your jacket?"

"It's right—" Lisa pointed to an empty chair just outside the employee lounge. "Oh, no! I left it on that chair a few minutes ago. It's gone!"

Ms. Long pushed Nancy aside and clapped her hands to get everyone's attention. "Another Morrell jacket is missing. It was the bright yellow one with the taxicab patch on the back. The shoplifter must have struck after locking me in the office."

"Maybe," said Nancy, "but maybe not. Maybe the alarm scared him or her off first."

"Or maybe in the confusion Lisa put it somewhere else. I'll check around the employee lounge and out front," Bess said, and left. Dan followed her.

"I hope you're right," Ms. Long called after them.

Nancy noticed that although the manager was furious she kept her voice low so the customers wouldn't hear. Ms. Long turned to Susan. "Go up front and take care of the customers. We don't want to scare them, and we can't afford to drive away business."

"Or," Nancy added half to herself, "to let them go without seeing if one of them has the jacket."

"Good thinking," Ms. Long said, then peered more closely at Nancy. "Do I know you?" she asked.

Nancy heard the note of suspicion in the manager's voice. She looked around for Bess to introduce her, but Bess was already out front with Dan. "My name is Nancy Drew. I'm one of Bess's friends."

Ms. Long looked relieved. "Nancy Drew?" She studied Nancy more closely. "I saw your picture in the paper a month or two back. You're Carson Drew's daughter, aren't you? I seem to remember that you're a bit of a crime solver. Maybe you can help here."

"I'd be glad to help," Nancy said, but before she could say more, Susan opened the door from the store.

"Security's here, Ms. Long," she called. "All the escalators stopped right after the alarm went off. And the stairs were jammed with people for the show."

So that's why they took so long to get here, Nancy thought. Ms. Long went onto the sales floor to meet the security person. Nancy took a moment to look around to see if whoever locked up the manager had left any clues. A quick check of the office and hallway turned up nothing suspicious. Nancy stopped long enough to see that the fire exit was closed and that the red toolbox Dan had used was perched beneath the electrical panel box on a shelf. She noted that it had "Property of Wicked" stenciled in black paint on the side.

When she came out front a few minutes later the store seemed to have returned to normal. Customers were going through racks of clothes. Susan and Kris were by the cash register. Lisa looked a little pale but was carefully going through the few remaining Morrell jackets, probably still hoping to find the missing yellow one.

As Nancy looked around for Bess, she saw Ms. Long walk back toward her office, followed by a young man with close-cut brown hair, wearing jeans and a Chicago Bulls sweatshirt. He was about twenty years old with high cheekbones and features too sharp to be conventionally handsome, but he looked intriguing. In fact, Nancy had trouble taking her eyes off him. She noticed the walkie-talkie he carried in one hand. If he's security, she thought, smiling inwardly, I'm looking forward to interviewing him for background on this case.

Nancy finally found Bess looking through a pile of slacks on a shelf. "Is that guy from security?" she asked. "He's not wearing a uniform."

"He's undercover, patrolling the stores for shoplifters," Bess told her. "His name is Frank Wexler." Nancy craned her neck as he disappeared into the back room. A big grin spread across Bess's face.

"Interested?"

"Who, me?" Nancy tried to laugh off the question but felt her cheeks grow warm. "Anything else stolen, besides the jacket?"

"No," Bess said. "I almost wish there was. This is getting freaky." Then she took Nancy's arm. "Nancy, I want you to meet Dan Schaffer."

The guy who had freed Ms. Long was standing a few feet away. "Dan," Bess went on, "this is Nancy Drew, the detective friend I told you about."

The guy looked hard at Nancy. She was sure she saw him start to blush, before he averted his face. All of a sudden he seemed terribly shy. "Hi," he mumbled.

"Nice to meet you, Dan," Nancy said with a smile, but Dan didn't return it. A thought tickled the back of Nancy's mind. She had a strange feeling she knew Dan from somewhere.

When Ms. Long came out of the back, Nancy noted Frank wasn't with her and felt a tiny twinge of disappointment.

"I'm sorry, Ms. Long," Bess said. "We've looked everywhere, but it's just not here."

"But only one jacket is missing," Lisa added glumly, as she joined them. "Mine."

"The alarm probably scared the thief before he or she could get to the others," Nancy surmised. "And of course the yellow jacket was easy to take since it wasn't tagged."

"The rest of the merchandise hasn't been touched," Bess said.

"I was pretty certain of that." Ms. Long shook her head. "Security went out the back to check the fire stairs, but we're sure the thief is long gone."

Ms. Long gestured for the girls to follow her back to the cash register, then waited until the customers were out of earshot. "Girls," she said quietly, "I've made a decision. I know this is a terrible disappointment, but I simply can't afford to leave the store shorthanded while that shoplifter is on the loose."

Ms. Long sighed, then spoke firmly. "I'm sorry, girls, but I'm pulling you from the show."

Chapter Three

"Ms. Long!" Bess and Lisa wailed in unison. Though Nancy could see the manager's point, she felt terrible for her friend. Bess's heart was set on modeling.

"I'm sorry." Ms. Long shook her head. "I need you all here, standing guard. I need—"

"Hello, everyone! I'm he-ere!" Heads turned as a loud trilling voice filled the store. It sounded like a strange cross between that of an opera singer and a valley girl.

When she saw the person who went with the voice, Nancy couldn't quite believe her eyes. On the woman's head stood a tall but droopy red- and white-striped top hat. Long, henna red banana curls streamed out from under it, squiggling down the woman's back all the way to her waist. Her legs looked like sticks in tight black stretch pants, and on top she wore what looked like a green velvet ringmaster's jacket. Multicolored wooden baubles clattered on her wrists as she extended her hand to Ms. Long, who reacted as if she were in total shock.

"I'm Mara Morrell," the woman said. "You must be Ms. Long."

"Yes, yes—of course." Ms. Long shook Mara's hand. "I'm so glad to meet you."

"Well, is everybody ready?" Mara Morrell asked, turning to the amateur models, clearly pleased to see them in their Morrell jackets and Lynxette wigs. "Come on! Let's go have a fashion show. Meet you on the runway." She whisked out the way she'd come in, like a summer storm out of the blue.

The girls all turned to Ms. Long, anxious to see if she was going to keep her word and forbid them to participate in the show.

Ms. Long's shoulders sagged, and Nancy could guess what she was thinking. The store owner was in a bind. If she kept the girls out of the fashion show, she'd risk offending the hottest new designer on the fashion scene. The Morrell jackets were hard enough to get as it was and annoying Mara wouldn't make it any easier. The girls held a single breath as Mara Morrell's distinctive voice trilled over the microphone on the runway. Over the cheers of the crowd Nancy could hear her begin to introduce herself and her spring line.

"Oh, go on," Ms. Long finally relented. "I'll watch the store by myself until you get back."

The girls all cheered. "Ms. Long?" said Lisa,

the one whose jacket had been taken. "What should I wear?"

The store manager frowned. "Oh, take another jacket from the rack. But guard it with your life!"

"Yes, Ms. Long."

The five Lynxette look-alikes rushed out of the store to join the professional models behind the curtain at the far end of the runway where a whole rack of Morrell original designs were ready for them. From the titters and squeals of delight coming from behind the curtain, Nancy could tell that this was a dream come true for them, particularly for Bess.

As the show was about to begin, Nancy threaded her way through the crowd and found George up in front, ready with her camera. Dan Schaffer was a few feet away. But when Nancy arrived, he shrank farther back into the crowd, once again avoiding her gaze.

"What was all the commotion?" George asked.

"Another Morrell jacket was shoplifted from Wicked," Nancy said, but she didn't want to say any more in earshot of Dan. There was something a little peculiar about him, at least about the way he acted around Nancy.

When Mara Morrell came out from behind the curtain—now in a hot pink strapless evening gown with a bush of pink organza sprouting from the thigh-high hem—she took the microphone and talked nonstop for the next half hour, describing the clothes and what she was trying to "say" with her fashions. To the beat of the dance music blasting from two huge speakers on the runway, the girls modeled the new designs. Bess was clearly having the time of her life, her smile getting broader and broader with each new outfit she wore.

Finally all the models came out together, swinging their hips to Lynxette's latest hit, "Money Talks," each one wearing a Mara Morrell jacket.

"Now for the moment you've all been waiting for," Mara announced as she slipped on a sapphire blue jacket with a red rose patch over her hot pink gown. "We're going to raffle off this jacket, which is one of the actual ones that was used in the 'Money Talks' video."

A ripple of excitement ran through the crowd. Female Lynxette fans clutched their raffle tickets anxiously, each one praying that she'd be the one to win the garment.

"Did you get a raffle ticket?" Nancy asked George.

"No. Morrell jackets aren't really my style," George said distractedly. She wasn't paying much attention to the fashion show. She kept looking back at the crowd. Nancy wondered if she was searching for the guy in the long tweed overcoat.

"You've got a point, George. It doesn't look like your kind of thing." Suddenly Nancy noticed that Dan was holding a ticket, and he looked as anxious as any of the girls in the audience. Why would he want a jacket, she wondered.

Up on the runway, Mara Morrell was reaching into her red- and white-striped hat, which was full of raffle ticket stubs. "And the lucky winner is—number one-seven-seven-three!"

"I won! I won!" someone screamed from the other side of the crowd. A girl with spiky black hair climbed onto the runway and half jogged toward the designer. Mara took off the sapphire blue jacket and helped the girl into it. "Congratulations!" Mara crowed into the mike. "Tell us your name and where you're from."

The girl was too excited to be shy. "My name is Lesley Richards," she said breathily, "and I'm from right here in River Heights."

"Do you know who she is?" Nancy asked George. "I don't remember seeing her at River Heights High."

"She goes to private school and is a year or two younger than we are," George said. "Her parents are friendly with my parents. She hangs out a lot at the mall."

"Well, that's it for the morning edition of my show," Mara quipped. "Unfortunately the jackets you just saw being modeled are some of the last ones left in River Heights. I guess they're just *too* popular. Though Wicked, the Jean Scene, and Chic Boutique still have a few left—if you hurry. I promise, though, that a new shipment will be coming as soon as we can get the factory to make them. Cross my heart. Bye-ee!"

Mara's trilling tones were still ringing in Nancy's ears when Bess worked her way through the crowd to her friends. "Did you get the pictures?" she asked George immediately.

"Yes, I got the pictures. I took the whole roll, just the way you wanted."

"Thanks! I can't wait to see them. Come on, let's take them down to the Photo Hut. Oh, here's Dan. Nancy, did you introduce him to George?"

George flashed Nancy a puzzled look, then turned to Dan. "Not yet." George poked her hand out in Dan's direction. Nancy watched as he smiled warmly at George and they introduced themselves.

"Uh, Bess," Dan said, leading Bess a couple of steps away. "Can I, ah, ask you something?"

"Of course, Dan. Is something wrong?" Nancy could hear their conversation still.

"No, no, nothing's wrong. I was just wondering if you could . . . Well, payday's not until Friday, and I'm a little broke—if you know what I mean."

"Oh, Dan," Bess said with a smile, "sure, I can lend you some money. That's not a problem."

"Can I borrow twenty dollars?"

Bess shrugged. "Sure, why not?"

Nancy was a little surprised to hear this. Twenty dollars was a lot of money to ask from someone who only worked part-time. Dan worked at CD City—why didn't he have his own money?

"Anyone else want to come to the Photo Hut?" Bess asked the others, taking Dan's hand. "None of the girls from Wicked are in the second half of Mara's show, but Ms. Long wants us to hurry back to the store."

"No, thanks," George said, as she handed the camera to Bess. "I need to check something out at Blazes and I want Nancy's opinion."

Nancy was puzzled but played along with her friend, eager to see what George was up to.

"Okay," Bess said. "I'll see you later then." She and Dan rushed off to take the escalator down to the lower level of the mall.

George looked a little sheepish as she turned to Nancy. "I had no luck tracking down the elusive Mr. X."

"And you want me to help you find him?"

"Well, I wouldn't say no if you offered, Nancy."

Nancy smiled at her friend. George had a bad case of love at first sight, she thought. "Tell you what," she said. "Let's do a quick sweep of the mall to see if we can find him. Maybe we'll get lucky."

George beamed. "Thanks, Nancy."

Nancy and George systematically combed the mall, starting on the upper level, then moving down to the lower level, hitting little boutiques as well as big department stores.

Other fashion shows were under way on other runways set up around the mall. But none of these were nearly so flashy or exciting as Mara Morrell's show.

When they passed CD City, just to the left of the atrium and fountain, Nancy noticed that the hardcore Lynxette fans were out in force, literally dancing in the aisles to "Money Talks." Obviously the rumor of Lynxette's appearance and possible video shoot later that week was spreading like wildfire.

As they wandered through the stores, Nancy was amazed to see how many kids were wearing Morrell jackets. It wasn't long before her head was spinning.

"George," she said. "Let's go to the food court and take a break. I'm starving."

"Me, too. After we eat, we'll be fueled up to search some more."

But as they headed toward the food court, Nancy happened to glance toward the upper level. Wicked's bright red and black sign was clearly visible. Then Nancy stopped and pointed. "George, look! Isn't that him?" Mr. X was coming out of Wicked, and he seemed to be in a big hurry.

"Come on, let's go," Nancy said, wondering what he had been doing in a women's clothing store. "Let's not lose him."

Nancy raced to the nearest staircase and bounded up the steps, two at a time. She and George arrived a minute later, breathless, on the upper level. They tried to catch up with the guy in the overcoat, but he had a long stride and quickly outdistanced them. Why was he in such a rush? Nancy wondered.

George seconded her thoughts. "I've never seen anyone in such a hurry to get to Davidson's," she remarked as they saw him turn into the huge department store nearby. They had barely set foot inside the store, when they noticed Mr. X making a left at the perfume counter and heading into the housewares department.

Nancy and George followed, but when they got to housewares the guy was nowhere to be found. The girls split up, scouring the aisles of coffee makers, pasta makers, microwave ovens, electric can openers, pots, pans, plates, and flatware. When they finally reunited, they couldn't figure out where he had gone. The housewares department was in a dead-end section of the store. Mr. X couldn't possibly have gotten past them.

"I don't get it," Nancy said.

George frowned, clearly frustrated that he'd gotten away. "Let's go back to Wicked. Maybe Bess saw him."

"If he bought something there and charged it, maybe we could find out his name."

George brightened. "Great idea, Nan. Except why would he shop in Wicked?" Her face fell. "Unless he's getting something for a friend—a girl friend."

Nancy laughed off George's concern. "Or a sister? Or mother?"

They headed back toward Wicked, weaving their way through the throngs of Lynxette-heads and mall rats that were gathered around the runway for the second half of Mara Morrell's fashion show.

As they approached the runway, Nancy wrinkled her nose. "George, do you smell something?"

George nodded. "Yes. It smells like something's burning."

Up on the runway, the microphone suddenly squealed to life. Mara Morrell was shielding her eyes from the spotlights and pointing down the hall in the direction of Purrs and Paws, the pet shop. "Oh—is that smoke?" she squeaked into the mike.

As if on cue the acrid smell in the air grew stronger, and Nancy's eyes began to burn. A second later a cloud of gray smoke billowed down the hall, blurring Nancy's vision.

"Fire!" someone screamed. Then panic seized the crowd and people ran shouting for the stairs and escalators to get down to the first floor.

Nancy grabbed for George but instead was caught up in the crowd and pushed down the hall toward the closest escalator—which was in the direction of the fire.

Chapter Four

NANCY FOUGHT to escape from the panicked crowd, but there was no way to keep from being pushed forward. Then suddenly, the crowd thinned out, and Nancy fell back against the wall just outside the entrance to Davidson's.

"No need to panic, folks!" a man's voice came over the mall's PA system. "Just a little trash can fire that was more smoke than fire. It's under control now."

Nancy rubbed at her eyes. She saw one of the sales clerks from Purrs and Paws lifting a fire extinguisher out of a large trash can. The fire was out, and someone had turned on the ventilation system. By the time George caught up to Nancy, the air was almost clear.

"Well"—Mara Morrell giggled into the mike as the crowd rapidly dispersed—"so much for the second half of our show. Bye-bye!"

Nancy frowned. It seemed like an inappropriate response to a fire, even if it was under control now.

"Come on, Nan," George said, brushing off her knapsack and straightening her shirt. "Let's go see what we can find out about Mr. X."

But when they walked into Wicked, Ms. Long was ruefully checking one of the sales racks. Bess and the other salesclerks' expressions were grim.

"I don't know what to do," Ms. Long complained. "If this keeps up we'll be out of business!"

"What's wrong?" Nancy asked.

Ms. Long sighed in frustration. "Another Morrell jacket is gone. A lime green one. The shoplifter has struck again!"

"Before we could notify security the fire started up," Bess said.

Another diversion, Nancy thought. Then her eyes met George's. George shook her head, and Nancy knew they were thinking the same thing. Just before Mr. X had pulled his vanishing act in Davidson's he'd come out of Wicked. He could certainly hide a jacket under that long coat he wore, Nancy thought. Could Mr. X be the shoplifter?

Just then Mara Morrell swept into the store. "Did you say another jacket was stolen? That's terrible." But from the tone of her voice she didn't sound disappointed.

"By any chance, Ms. Long, do you have any chilled mineral water?" Mara asked, fanning her face with her hand. "I'm absolutely parched from that smoke."

Nancy frowned. There was something very peculiar about Mara Morrell, she thought to herself.

Obviously Ms. Long thought so, too. "Ms. Morrell," she said, "why don't you send one of your crew downstairs for the water? I don't have any, and I have to get security up here. These thefts are getting more and more serious."

"Oh, sure." Mara waved breezily in Ms. Long's direction. "Sorry about the theft. Ta!" With that she walked out of the store.

"That woman," Ms. Long muttered, barely loud enough for Nancy to hear.

Nancy shook her head, then turned back to Ms. Long. "Why didn't the security system kick in when the thief made off with the jacket?"

Ms. Long pushed her hair back and rubbed her temples. "I can't figure it." She led Nancy over to the cash register and held up the slim two-pronged security deactivation wand. "You simply can't remove the tag without this gadget. . . ." Suddenly Ms. Long stopped speaking, her face registering panic. She yanked open a small drawer hidden beneath the counter. Her big eyes widened. "Our back-up wand—it's not here!" she exclaimed.

At that moment Frank Wexler walked into the store. Nancy was embarrassed to feel her heart give a little flip-flop. She stepped back, glad for a moment that Frank wasn't looking her way.

"What's the problem, Ms. Long? I just got a call on my radio."

"It's happened again, Frank."

Frank shook his head and pulled out a notepad from his back pocket. "Another of those jackets?"

"I'm afraid so," Ms. Long said. "And I just found out our backup deactivation wand is missing. I'm not sure how long it's been gone. I can't believe I didn't think to check before."

Frank frowned. "This thief knows what he or she is doing," he said. "It's beginning to sound like an inside job." He opened his notepad and took out a pen. "Give me all the details. Maybe the thief left a clue."

Nancy couldn't stop watching him. She liked his take-charge attitude and his deep baritone voice.

As Ms. Long gave her statement to Frank Wexler, George pulled Nancy and Bess aside. "Bess, did you happen to notice a tall guy wearing a long tweed overcoat in here. It would have been just before the fire?"

Bess scrunched her mouth to one side and thought about it. "That description doesn't ring a bell. Not many guys come in here."

George nodded. "Nancy and I figured that. But we really did see him coming out of here."

"Maybe I was in the back. Check with the other girls, George."

"Bess, do you think it would be all right if I looked around the store?" Nancy asked.

"If it'll help us stop the shoplifter, I'm sure Ms. Long wouldn't mind."

"Thanks."

Nancy decided to make a systematic study of the store. First she checked the dressing rooms. They were empty. No jackets in sight.

Then she headed for the back, determined to check the area more carefully. The space was divided into several rooms, opening off the narrow hallway. One door was marked Storeroom. Nancy tried the handle and found it locked. Another door led to the employee lounge where Bess had gotten ready for the show that morning. The third was Ms. Long's office.

Nancy moved down the hall to the emergency exit. It had a dead bolt as well as a regular key lock, but the bolt was thrown open. Nancy wondered if this was normal. Maybe they locked the dead bolt from the inside only when the store was closed for the night.

Nancy opened the door cautiously, hoping she wouldn't set off an alarm. But apparently any alarms had already been turned off. Nancy wondered when and by whom. Seeing that she'd need a key to get back in, Nancy was careful not to let the door close behind her, as she peered into the rear corridor. It was empty and all the back doors to the other stores were closed. If the thief had gone out this way, he or she was long gone, Nancy concluded.

She heaved a sigh and closed the door, then headed back to the employee lounge. She hated to suspect any of Wicked's employees, especially since they were all Bess's friends. But it was a known fact that employees can and do shoplift. Nancy hesitated outside the lounge. Though solving crimes was her passion, she hated putting innocent people under suspicion.

Nancy blew out her breath, shouldered her bag, and reached for the doorknob. It would be better to find out right away than to let suspicions linger.

She poked her head inside. "Hello? Is anyone here? Oh!"

A guy in a khaki shirt was standing near the row of gray lockers. He had a brown plastic garbage bag slung over his shoulder. He was very blond, with crystal blue eyes, a trim build, and fair skin.

"Hi," he said. His face colored slightly.

"Oh, hi." Nancy tried to act as natural as possible, though she was surprised to find a guy in the lounge. "I was just looking for—"

"Stop! Thief!" a deep voice cried from the hallway outside.

The guy stepped back against the bank of lockers. He looked first to the right and then to the left, where Nancy stood blocking the door.

For a moment Nancy thought she saw fear in his eyes.

Before she could finish the thought, Frank Wexler pushed into the room, and grabbed Nancy by the arm. His grip gave her an unexpected tingle that made her blush.

"Wait! Let me explain." Nancy tried to pull away, but Frank Wexler was very strong.

Ms. Long rushed in. "Oh, Frank. No," she cried "That's Nancy Drew. Bess's friend. She's helping me investigate the burglaries. I haven't had a chance to introduce you."

Bess and George appeared behind Ms. Long. George's eyes widened as she took in the scene. Nancy almost laughed at the expression on her face.

"Frank," Bess gasped. "Nancy's no thief."

"Sorry," Frank said, letting go of her arm. "I just thought—"

"It's all right," Nancy said. "You were just doing your job." Frank averted his gaze, though a funny smile played about his lips.

The boy in the khaki shirt shifted the garbage bag to his other shoulder. "Excuse me folks. If everything's okay here, I'll be getting back to garbage duty," he said.

"Sure, Craig," Frank said, stepping aside to let him pass.

Nancy looked from Frank to Craig's back as he walked out the back door. She noticed that Craig had a set of keys dangling from a ring on his belt. If he worked in mall maintenance it made sense he was in the lounge picking up the garbage, she supposed, and also that he knew his way around the back halls.

"Can we finish up that report now, Ms. Long?" Frank asked, flashing an apologetic smile at Nancy.

"Yes, yes. Let's go into my office."

As soon as they left, Nancy turned to Bess. "Who was that guy in the khaki shirt? Why didn't Ms. Long think *he* was the thief?"

"His name is Craig Jordan," Bess said. "He works part-time for the mall maintenance department." From the way Bess spoke, Nancy knew there was more to the story.

"His family is *very* rich," Bess continued. "In fact, his father is a part-owner of the mall. But he's very strict, and he wants his son to learn his version of old-fashioned values. That's why he makes Craig work here for his spending money." She lowered her voice. "From what I've heard, Craig and his father don't get along very well."

"Hmmm . . ." Nancy mulled this over for a minute. Somehow father-son problems didn't seem a likely motive for shoplifting. She headed for the door.

"Where are you going?" George asked.

"I want to talk to Frank Wexler. I want to find out what he knows about all of these shopliftings. Do you want to come?"

George and Bess exchanged knowing glances.

"Is this professional curiosity?" George asked.

"Or is it a case of romantic interest?" Bess gave Nancy a sly wink. "Is Frank about to give Ned some competition?"

Nancy crossed her arms and tried to suppress a smile. She failed miserably. "I'm only interested in catching this shoplifter. That's all," she said with a laugh.

"Yeah, right," the cousins said in unison.

"I'm going skating," George called to her.

Thinking of Frank and Ned, Nancy left the employee lounge and headed for Ms. Long's office. Ned, she thought, was causing her confusion lately. He had been her boyfriend for a long time, but was now off at Emerson College. Lately they had both agreed that dating other people made sense. But as cute as Frank Wexler was, he didn't hold a candle to Ned, whom Nancy had known forever and counted among her very best friends.

Ms. Long's office door was open. The manager was at her desk—alone.

"Is Frank Wexler still here?"

"I'm afraid not, Nancy," Ms. Long said. "He got a call on his radio, and had to run. Try the Jean Scene, down on the lower level."

"Thanks, Ms. Long." Nancy hurried out of the store, hoping to catch up with him.

The first thing that Nancy noticed when she walked into the Jean Scene was that it wasn't as sophisticated as Wicked. It sold both men's and women's clothing, and specialized in jeans, T-shirts, oversize tops, and sweatshirts.

Nancy scanned the busy store, looking for Frank Wexler. A bunch of high school kids were joking and laughing loudly in the changing room stalls that lined one wall. The opposite wall was stocked with shelves of jeans in various cuts and colors.

Glancing in one of the many mirrors, Nancy suddenly spotted the reflection of Bess's new boyfriend, Dan Schaffer. He was looking through a rack of half-price plaid flannel shirts.

"Hi, Dan," Nancy said.

Dan looked up, surprised. His expression turned grim when he recognized Nancy. "Oh—hi," he muttered, and immediately averted his eyes. "Gotta go." With that, he turned and walked out of the store.

Nancy didn't know what to make of this. Dan had seemed a little unfriendly before, but now it was clear that Nancy made him very uncomfortable. She couldn't imagine why.

Nancy finally spotted Frank at the back of the store, talking to a young man with long dreadlocks. As Nancy walked that way, she noticed four or five Morrell jackets on the rack next to them, all bunched together.

"Yeah, these are the last ones we have," the man was saying to Frank. As she drew closer, Nancy noted he wore a Jean Scene employee ID tag. "But with all the people here for Fashion Week, I'm having a hard time watching the store." He frowned and nodded at the mall rats horsing around near the changing stalls. "I was hoping maybe you could post a guard outside until things got back to normal."

Frank shook his head. "I wish I could help you out, Reggie, but we're spread pretty thin as it is. We've got all our guards working double shifts this week just to handle the crowds."

"Hi, Frank," Nancy said, coming up to them.

"Oh, hi, Nancy." The sparkle in Frank's eye when he noticed her made her feel great.

"I didn't mean to interrupt, but can I talk to you when you're finished here?" Nancy asked.

"Sure," Frank said. "I was going for a snack at the food court after this. Will you join me?"

"I'd love to," Nancy said. "I'll just browse around the store until you're ready."

Nancy wandered a few feet away to check out the sweatshirts. She could still hear Reggie and Frank's conversation and was surprised to learn that Jean Scene had recently switched to the same kind of security system as Wicked. Chaining the valuable jackets made more sense to Nancy.

Reggie continued to make his case for extra security at his store, complaining that he'd already lost quite a few Morrell jackets. This really was a serious problem, Nancy thought. Then Reggie mentioned that Mara Morrell refused to sell jackets to stores that chained them. "Ruins their free, wild image," he said in disgust.

Nancy raised her eyebrows. Either Mara

Morrell was the biggest flake Nancy had ever encountered, or she had some ulterior motive for making her jackets so accessible. Nancy unfolded a sweatshirt to look at the design on the front. She wasn't surprised to see a picture of Lynxette in the gold Morrell jacket she'd worn in the "Money Talks" video.

"Nancy?" Frank was walking toward her. "We can go now—"

Nancy took a step toward him, then could go no farther. Something—or someone—had blacked out the lights. The store was in total darkness.

Nancy reached out, feeling in front of her. Suddenly she felt strong fingers gripping hers. "It's me, Nancy. Frank."

Frank squeezed her hand, and Nancy couldn't help but squeeze back. "What's happening?" she whispered, not quite sure why she was keeping her voice down. The kids in the changing stalls were screaming and giggling hysterically.

Before Frank could answer, Nancy heard a shout from the back of the store. "Hey!" Reggie yelled. "What do you think you're doing? Oowww!"

Nancy heard a loud thud, then something heavy hitting the floor. It sounded like a body falling.

Chapter Five

"GET DOWN," Frank commanded in a whisper. He pulled Nancy to the floor, keeping a hand on her back. Nancy felt her pulse racing.

"Stay here," Frank said. "I'm going to—"

Just then the lights flickered back on. Nancy and Frank scrambled to their feet. Nancy instantly bolted to the back of the store to see what had happened to Reggie. Frank was close on her heels. They found Reggie sitting on the floor, clutching his head, rocking back and forth in pain.

"Reggie, hey, are you all right?" Frank knelt beside him.

"No, I'm not all right." When Reggie lifted his face toward them, they could see a bruise already taking color on his forehead. "Someone bashed me over the head."

"Look!" Nancy pointed at the rack of jackets. The five Morrell jackets were gone.

"Unbelievable!" Reggie cried, trying to struggle to his feet. He winced and sat down again heavily. "Those stupid Morrell jackets are more trouble than they're worth." He rubbed his head, then suddenly exclaimed. "Hey! What happened to the alarm?"

"It should have gone off when the lights did," Frank remarked worriedly. He tapped the On switch on his two-way radio. While he spoke to the security office, Nancy sat with Reggie and told him about the security wand that was missing from Wicked.

"I'm going to check the back room," Frank said, as he clicked off his walkie-talkie. "And talk to those kids, in case anyone saw anything. Not that I have much hope—even security cameras can't see in the dark." He put a hand on Reggie's shoulder. "You just take it easy, buddy. Lie still until we can get an ambulance here."

Nancy helped Reggie lie back, taking a jean jacket from the nearest rack and bunching it up to make a pillow for the back of his head.

Frank turned to Nancy and smiled wryly. "I'm afraid I'll have to take a rain check on that snack," he said.

"I understand," she answered. "Do what you have to do. I'm going to check back at Wicked to make sure everything's okay there."

"Good idea," Frank said. "But, Nancy, I do want to get together sometime and talk—and not just about the case."

"Me, too." Despite the recent scare, Nancy was grinning. She would definitely be looking forward to seeing Frank again.

Suddenly two uniformed security guards ran into the store with a first-aid kit. While they attended to Reggie, Frank headed for the back room.

Having made sure Reggie was taken care of, Nancy stepped out into the atrium of the mall and tried to sort out her thoughts. This Morrell jacket craze was getting even crazier.

As Nancy took the escalator to the upper level, a panoramic view of the lower level opened up before her. There were runways set up on both sides of the central court, each one hosting a different fashion show—sportswear on one side, evening wear on the other. Each side had its own music: rap for the jeans and sneakers; Broadway show tunes for the full-length gowns. The people down below grew smaller as she drifted up higher, but dotting the crowd, like colorful paint spatters in an abstract painting, were the ever-present rainbow colors of Mara Morrell's enormously popular jackets. Nancy couldn't help but wonder how many of them were stolen and how many purchased legitimately.

She got off the escalator and headed for Wicked. When she got there, she saw the whole staff huddled together by the cash register. Ms. Long was standing with her arms crossed and her lips pursed. As Nancy approached, she heard Bess exclaiming over the latest theft at the Jean Scene. The news had traveled fast.

Nancy waited until the group broke up before cornering Bess.

"No more Morrell jackets have been stolen from Wicked, have they?" Nancy asked. Bess shook her head glumly. "How many do you have left?"

"Just one," Bess said, "and Ms. Long's saving it for her kid sister." She pointed to a mannequin wearing a candy-apple red jacket with a dancing bear cub on the back. "We just sold the others."

"Ms. Long should take that one home before it's stolen," Nancy suggested.

Bess shook her head. "She promised Mara Morrell she'd leave it on display for Fashion Week. But the way things are going, I doubt that it'll survive the week." Bess breathed a sigh. "She's threatening to pull us out of the remaining shows if the thief isn't caught soon."

"I don't see the point. What can you do?" Nancy commiserated. "This thief is smart and seems to know how to overcome security precautions—"

"It gets worse." Bess sighed heavily as she leaned against a wall beside a display of stretchy leggings in bright colors. "Dan just told me we're scheduled to be onstage with Lynxette when she comes to film her video on Friday. How can Ms. Long keep us from being part of that? It's the chance of a lifetime!"

"Speaking of Dan—" Nancy was still puzzled by Dan's unfriendly behavior. "I need to talk to you about him."

Bess was oblivious to Nancy's request.

"I wish that stupid shoplifter would go to some other mall," she said. "I mean, I was saving up to buy one of those jackets. I hadn't decided which one I liked better—the olive or the lavender—but now it doesn't matter. There are none left."

"Bess, I want to ask you about—"

"I liked the lavender one because of the color, but I preferred the palm tree patch that was on the olive one. It would have been a tough choice."

"Bess, can we talk about something else for a minute?"

"You know, Nancy, the one I *really* wanted was that sapphire blue one with the red rose patch that Lesley Richards won."

"Bess—"

"Lesley's so lucky to have won it. It's one of the best combinations I've ever seen in a Morrell jacket. Now I don't know what I'm going to do. Of course by the time I save up enough money, there probably won't be a single jacket left for sale in River Heights, and you heard what Mara Morrell said at the fashion show—she doesn't know when the next shipment will be ready."

"Bess, tell me something. How did you meet Da—?"

"Of course, maybe the new batch will be *better* than the old ones, in which case I'll be the one who lucks out because I waited. Then again, they won't be the same as the ones that'll be in the Lynxette video we're going to be filming, so I really don't know what's better. What do you think, Nancy?"

Nancy could only sigh. It was no use trying to get Bess to think about anything other than Morrell jackets. But that got Nancy to thinking about Dan again. The jackets cost about seventy dollars, not exactly cheap. Dan Schaffer only worked part-time, and he couldn't be making all that much at CD City. On top of that, he even borrowed money from Bess the other day. Could he be the one stealing the Morrell jackets? Nancy had seen him leaving the Jean Scene just before the lights went out. Could he be working with an accomplice?

Nancy decided to give it one more try with her friend. "Bess, listen to me. The last time you and Dan went out, what did you do? Where did you go?"

Bess's eyes brightened. "We went out last Saturday night. Oh, it was so special, Nancy. You'll never guess where he took me. We went to—"

"Nancy! Bess!" George burst into Wicked as if she were dashing for the finish line in the marathon.

"What is it? What's wrong?"

"Lesley Richards—" George said, out of breath. "I just found out—she was mugged!"

Chapter Six

NANCY COULDN'T BELIEVE her ears. "Lesley Richards was mugged? When, George?"

George was still trying to catch her breath. "This morning . . . in the parking lot . . . right after Mara Morrell's show. The mugger took her Morrell jacket."

Nancy was skeptical. "In broad daylight? That's kind of hard to believe."

Bess disagreed. "Not true, Nancy. Ask anyone who works here. There's at least one mugging here each week, sometimes during the day—especially when it's extra busy. The farthest parking spaces are almost a third of a mile from the nearest entrance."

"And out of sight of security," George remarked.

"Sure," Bess said. "Muggers wait in their cars. After they strike they can get away fast.

By the time the victim gets back to the mall to call for help, the mugger is long gone."

Nancy shook her head in dismay. "Was Lesley hurt? Did security call the police?"

George frowned. "I don't know about security. I heard about this from one of the kids over at the roller rink. He ran into Lesley an hour ago in the arcade. He said she seemed okay."

"That's good," Nancy said, but she couldn't help thinking that if she had been mugged she wouldn't be in an arcade playing video games a couple of hours later. Her gaze drifted to the last Morrell jacket in Wicked, the candy-apple red one on the mannequin at the front of the store. "This mugging could be connected to the shoplifting spree," she said, thinking out loud. "Burglaries are bad, but muggings are so much worse—Lesley could have been seriously hurt." Nancy thought of Reggie holding his bruised head at the Jean Scene.

"What are you going to do, Nancy?" Bess asked.

"George, I want you to go find Frank Wexler. I wonder if he knows about the mugging. Meanwhile, I want to talk to Lesley myself. Do you think she's still around the mall?"

George shrugged. "If she is, she's probably at the arcade. She hangs with a group of mall rats who spend half their lives there."

"Okay," Nancy said, tucking her shirt more securely into her jeans. She backed out of the store and promised, "I'll see you two later."

Nancy headed for the escalator and hurried down the moving stairs to the lower level. The arcade was the first storefront past the food court. As she threaded her way past the lines of customers, tempting aromas mingled in her nose. Small tables and chairs covered an area half the size of a basketball court where shoppers sipped drinks and snacked. Fast-food concessions lined the edges of the food court, one right after the other: Mamma Mia's Pizza, Hound Dog Foot-Long Wieners, the Seafood Dock, Roly-Poly Stuffed Potatoes, Sergeant Garcia's Taco Junction, House of Wu Chinese Delights, and on and on and on. Nancy passed the gourmet popcorn stand, which had popcorn in more colors than the Morrell jackets, and arrived at Arcade Animals.

Nancy stepped inside and waited for her eyes to adjust to the lower light level. The lights were turned down to minimize the glare in the video screens, but it made the arcade seem a little creepy.

Because of the fashion shows that day, the arcade was crowded with kids. Nancy walked by a new video game she hadn't seen before and wished she had time to try it out. She smiled to herself, thinking that it would be fun to challenge Frank to a game when he had a break. She wondered if he'd go for it. She shook off the thought—at the moment she had to concentrate on finding Lesley and asking her a few questions while the mugging was still fresh in her mind.

In a back corner some scruffier-looking teens were hanging out by a big blue machine near the arcade's fire exit.

"Hey, get a load of Ms. Preppie!" one of the guys commented as she passed. Nancy glanced up. The guy's head was shaved, but he sported a day's worth of stubble on his chin.

"She's probably here for a Morrell makeover," chided a girl with a nose ring.

"She sure needs one!" another girl in a silver Morrell jacket laughed.

Inwardly Nancy concocted a few choice comebacks. But she didn't need trouble now, so she kept her mouth shut and moved on.

She peered into the shadows, intent on finding Lesley and trying not to stare at some of the more creatively dressed game players. The garish colors of the Morrell jackets worn by some of the girls just added to the bizarre atmosphere of the arcade.

At first she didn't see Lesley. But when she looked into the corner behind the last video game in the row, she found a boy and a girl locked in an embrace, passionately kissing. The boy's blond head was turned away from Nancy, but she recognized the slender girl whose arms were wrapped around his neck. Lesley's spiky black hair and row of silver bracelets were distinctive. Nancy hung back, not wanting to interrupt such an intimate moment. But Lesley's mugging was serious, and Nancy needed to learn the details.

"Lesley?"

The startled couple parted to see who was there. Nancy's jaw dropped when she saw the guy. It was Craig Jordan, who worked for the maintenance department.

"Sorry." Nancy smiled sheepishly. "Didn't mean to interrupt." Craig sure gets around, Nancy thought to herself. This had to be a secret relationship, or else Bess would have known about it.

Craig acted confused but seemed to recognize Nancy. Nancy couldn't read the expression in his clear blue eyes. "I'll call you tonight," he said to Lesley, and abruptly walked away.

"Lesley, I'm Nancy Drew, Bess Marvin's friend—"

"I don't care who you are," Lesley said, straightening her sweater. Her pale cheeks were pink, and she seemed to be flustered. Up close Lesley was really beautiful, Nancy thought, even with her dyed black hair and row of delicate silver earrings studding her left ear. She had long dark eyelashes, and her deep-set eyes were huge—at the moment, it seemed, with fear. Nancy tilted her head and studied Lesley carefully. Maybe she was still freaked out from the mugging.

"You've got to promise me," Lesley said, panic expressed on her face, "promise me that you won't tell *anyone* that you saw me with Craig. My parents would kill me if they found out."

Now Nancy was more curious than ever. "Why? Don't they like Craig?"

"My father can't stand Craig or his father, either. They're business rivals."

Nancy nodded, taking this all in. Bess had mentioned that Lesley was from a wealthy family, just like Craig. But she hadn't said the families were feuding.

"Don't worry," Nancy assured Lesley. "I won't tell a soul about you and Craig. What I'm worried about is the fact that you were mugged this morning."

Lesley stiffened slightly. "What about it?"

"Well, I'm investigating the Morrell jacket shopliftings here at the mall. Since you were mugged for your Morrell jacket, I'm wondering if there may be a connection. Was that the only thing that the mugger took?"

"Uh, no." Leslie sounded hesitant.

"What else did he get?"

"My purse."

"Did you get a good look at him?"

"No," Leslie said, her voice a little stronger this time. "He came up from behind."

"Did he have a gun or a knife?"

"I don't—I don't think so. But he stuck something in my back to scare me."

Nancy's heart stopped—if the mugger was the thief he had suddenly upped the ante. He was playing for keeps. Were the jackets *that* valuable? Suddenly Nancy realized she had forgotten to ask a very important question.

"This mugger who threatened you—it was a guy?"

"Yes, of course." Lesley screwed up her face. "Uh—I mean, I could tell by his voice," she added quickly. "A guy's voice—definitely."

"What did he say?"

"I don't remember."

"How'd he get away? On foot or in a car?"

"How am I supposed to know?" Lesley was beginning to act impatient. She peered past Nancy's shoulder and fiddled with one of her tiny earrings. "You know, I was scared. I wasn't paying much attention—" The panicky note was back in her voice.

Nancy had conducted difficult interviews before, but this one was like pulling teeth.

"Did you report the incident to the police?" She tried again.

"What good would that do? They never catch these guys. Anyway," Lesley added, "I don't think my being mugged has anything to do with the shoplifting spree. You're wasting your time talking to me."

"I'm not so sure about that," Nancy said. "And if I were you, I'd go to the police. It's true, they may not get your stuff back, but if you could help them track down the guy, other girls with Morrell jackets won't get mugged."

Lesley rolled her eyes. "Believe me. Cops never catch the real crooks."

"Well, if *you* don't report this, maybe I will."

"No!" Lesley stepped up to Nancy and

glared. "It's my stuff that was ripped off. This is none of your business, so stay out of it. Or—or else."

Nancy couldn't believe what she was hearing. "Are you threatening me?"

"Take it any way you want." Lesley brushed past her and left the arcade, squeezing past a trio of guys who had gathered to hear what was going on.

"You heard what Lesley said," the guy with the shaved head said. "You better mind your own business. . . ."

Suddenly Nancy realized that she was backed into a corner—a wall on one side, a bulky video game on the other. And three tough guys closing in on her.

Chapter Seven

THE GUY with the shaved head stepped closer to Nancy and put a hand on the wall behind her.

The other two guys played backup.

Nancy forced herself to calm down and focus, so she could think. Even though she knew karate, there were three guys, and three against one were tough odds.

"So what's the story, babe?" the guy with the shaved head taunted. "You going to leave Lesley alone or take us all on?"

Nancy didn't answer. Anything she said would just rile him.

"Cat got your tongue?" The second guy jeered. The other two joined in his laughter.

"All right, break it up!" Suddenly Frank Wexler appeared behind the three guys, who took one look at him—and the hefty nightstick hanging from his belt—and slunk off out of the arcade. Frank turned to watch them go, his strong arms folded across his chest. He looked back over his shoulder. "Are you all right, Nancy?" he asked.

"I'm okay," Nancy said. "But I'm sure glad you turned up." Nancy often found herself in unnerving situations and rarely had trouble fending for herself. But looking up at Frank just then, she decided being rescued once in a while was something she could get used to.

Frank regarded Nancy steadily. Nancy was surprised she hadn't noticed his large gray eyes before. For a brief instant their eyes locked. Then Frank shifted his gaze to his hands and spoke softly. "You're pretty cool under pressure, Nancy Drew."

Nancy couldn't help hearing the admiration in his voice. She began to crack a smile. "I have to confess, I *am* pretty good at karate."

Frank blew out his breath in a whistle. "Not to mention a very interesting person."

"Thank you—I think," Nancy flirted.

Frank's smile widened for a moment, then his face grew serious. "Good thing one of the kids came out and told me there was trouble brewing in the arcade. Frankly, Nancy, this isn't the safest place in the mall. We have trouble down here all the time."

"I can see why." The three guys were still hanging around, peering in from outside.

"Your friend George just told me about

Lesley Richard's mugging. Is that who you were down here trying to find?" Frank asked.

"I found her," Nancy said. "But I couldn't get much out of her." She quickly summed up her conversation with Lesley.

"It does sound a little odd," Frank agreed. "I'll see if I can have someone from security talk to her. Have you uncovered anything else?"

"Not much," Nancy said, shaking her head. She hesitated, afraid of casting suspicion on someone innocent. Still, Mr. X's disappearing act before the fire bothered her. "There is one thing—I saw a guy—tall, about six-foot-two, wearing a long, vintage tweed overcoat. He came out of Wicked just before it was burgled. Maybe it's nothing—but the fire started just after he vanished. I've got nothing concrete, but—"

"I understand, Nancy. I'll keep my eye out for him, in case he's still hanging around. Not many guys shop in Wicked."

Just then Frank's walkie-talkie crackled. "I've got to run," he said, after speaking to his security chief. "Let me walk you out of the arcade."

When they reached the food court, Frank hung back, seeming reluctant to leave. "Maybe tomorrow we can get together," he said. "And take a few minutes to talk."

"I'd love that," Nancy said, with a smile. Frank backed away a few steps, returning her grin, then turned around and jogged off. Nancy hated to see him go.

The next day was sunny, cool, and breezy. Nancy arrived at the mall parking lot early, intent on making progress with her investigation. So far she hadn't any concrete evidence. All she did have were three suspects whose only crime was their suspicious behavior: unfriendly Dan Schaffer who was in the Jean Scene just before the blackout; Mara Morrell, whose reaction to the thefts at Wicked was very odd indeed; and Mr. X, who was seen coming out of Wicked right after one of the shoplifting incidents. The thief could be anyone really, Nancy thought, as she pulled her blue Mustang into an empty parking space about a hundred feet from the loading dock behind Davidson's Department Store. A big trailer truck was parked in the last bay.

Nancy was just about to get out of the car when she saw someone emerge from the shadows on the loading dock. It was Craig Jordan, wearing his khaki shirt under a shearling jacket, a brown plastic garbage bag slung over his shoulder. Nancy watched from her car as he dropped the garbage bag into a small Dumpster behind the truck bay. Everything seemed normal enough.

Craig then went over to the back of the trailer truck and slipped inside. Nancy straightened up in her seat, but from where she was parked she couldn't see what he was doing. A moment later Craig emerged and disappeared into the shadows of the loading dock.

Nancy jumped out of the Mustang and hurried past the lines of parked cars toward the loading dock. She wanted to catch up with Craig before he went back in, so she could ask him what he knew about Lesley's mugging. She started to mount the loading dock steps, then stopped when she heard footsteps coming out of the shadows. It wasn't Craig, though. It was Mr. X in his long tweed overcoat!

Mr. X didn't seem to notice her. Nancy watched as he headed toward the rear of the truck. She backed down the steps and slipped into the shadow of the trailer, listening carefully. A moment later she heard his footsteps inside.

Nancy waited for what seemed an eternity. Finally Mr. X stepped out of the truck and backed onto the loading dock. She soon heard a heavy door open and slam shut. Mr. X had gone back into the mall.

Cautiously, Nancy slipped out of the shadow of the truck and hurried up the steps onto the loading dock. She stood before the open rear of the truck and peered inside, her eyes gradually adjusting to the dim light. It was full of large cardboard boxes stacked on pallets. According to the printing on the boxes, they were partially assembled lawn mowers. What did Craig and Mr. X want with lawn mowers?

But maybe there weren't just lawn mowers, she thought as she ventured inside. Could there also be a shipment of Morrell jackets somewhere in there?

Nancy moved deeper into the trailer. It was colder than she'd expected, so she zipped up her wool baseball jacket. What *were* Craig and Mr. X both doing in here? She was about to turn back when she stepped on something. Nancy saw that it was a small black leather backpack.

Curious, she picked it up and crouched down behind a stack of boxes to inspect it in case Craig or Mr. X came back. At the bottom of the pack was a matching black leather wallet. She looked inside but found no cash or credit cards and no ID of any kind. Nancy kept searching, though, and her persistence paid off. Crammed deep into an inside compartment of the wallet, she found an old library card—issued to Lesley Richards.

Nancy's brain started to race with possible reasons for Lesley's backpack being there.

If Mr. X was the person who mugged Lesley for her Morrell jacket, he might have come back here to get rid of the incriminating pack and wallet. Muggers usually just take the cash and credit cards and discard the rest. Mr. X might have thought tossing the pack in the back of a truck was an ingenious idea. The truck could be hundreds of miles away before it was discovered.

But why had Craig come here? Was it possible that he and Mr. X were working together? But would Craig really go along with a plan to mug Lesley? She was his girlfriend, after all.

Nancy picked up the backpack and checked it again for anything that might help her figure things out. Turning the pack completely inside out, she found a hidden inside pocket. She unzipped it and felt around. Her fingers closed around a small book.

She pulled it out and discovered it was a tiny tan address book. She flipped to the first page. "If Lost Please Return to Lesley Richards, 44 Pearl Road, River Heights, Illinois."

Nancy flipped through a few more pages at random. There were names and phone numbers of people she didn't know. But when she got to the *S* page, she was surprised to find Dan Schaffer's name and phone number, circled in bright red pen.

Dan and Lesley went to different schools—Nancy hadn't thought they even knew each other. Why would Dan's name be circled in red? Nancy hated to consider the possibility, but could Dan be cheating on Bess with Lesley? Did he always act so unfriendly around Nancy because he knew she was one of Bess's best friends and was good at getting to the bottom of things? But if Lesley were dating Dan, why would she have been kissing Craig?

Nancy was beginning to get a headache trying to sort out all the questions she had. She leaned back against the wall of the trailer and started to massage her temples when suddenly she heard the rear gate of the truck bang shut. Instantly, Nancy was entombed in darkness.

"Lock it up, Bob," she heard a man say. "We have to get going."

"Be right with you, Tim," another man said.

The engine rumbled to life then, so loud that she could barely hear the clank as the padlock on the back door was locked.

Nancy stood up, reaching out with both hands in the darkness. "Help!" she cried. But as the engine revved up, a loud rumbling sound drowned out her voice.

Nancy started to take a step, but at the same moment the truck lurched forward, throwing her back into a stack of boxes. She regained her balance and tried to get her bearings. Then she smelled something. With horror, Nancy realized what the deafening rumble must mean. A broken muffler! She had to get out—and fast. Exhaust fumes were already seeping into the trailer of the semi.

"Help!" she shouted. "Stop the truck!"

It was no use. No one could hear her.

Nancy started to cough. Panic overcame her. What if they were heading for the highway, starting out on a long trip? She wouldn't survive long back there, not with noxious exhaust leaking in. She tried to shout again, but the fumes got to her, and she couldn't stop coughing. She covered her mouth with her sleeve, tears streaming down her face. It was no use. The driver and his helper wouldn't realize she was back here until it was too late. Nancy was trapped!

Chapter Eight

MUSTERING EVERY OUNCE of her strength, Nancy fought her way through the dark to the front of the trailer and started pounding on the wall closest to the cab of the truck. She pried off her ankle boot and hammered the wall with its heel.

"Please!" she cried. "Please help! You've *got* to hear me!"

Nancy banged harder, willing herself on despite the fumes. Then suddenly she was thrown into the front wall as the truck screeched to a halt. A few moments later the back gate of the trailer rolled up, and sunlight flooded the darkness. A wave of cool, fresh air washed over Nancy's face. She took a deep, shaky breath.

"Hey in there! Are you all right?" a burly guy holding a set of keys in one hand called into the trailer. Nancy figured he must be the driver.

"What're you doing in there?" his partner asked in a voice that sounded half-annoyed, half-astounded.

As Nancy stumbled to the end of the trailer, she started coughing again. "It's a long story. . . . It was an accident. . . . You closed up the truck while I was inside."

"What were you doing in there in the first place?" the partner asked. He was about twenty-five years old and very skinny, his dark hair pulled back in a short ponytail. "Were you trying to steal something?"

"No." Nancy shook her head. "My name is Nancy Drew, and I was looking for the truck-load sale," she fibbed, not knowing if these men were involved somehow in the jacket scam or Lesley's mugging. "Davidson's Department Store is supposed to be having a truckload sale today."

"Well, you've got the wrong truck," the young guy said.

Nancy wriggled into her boot and hopped down out of the truck. To her amazement they had gotten only to the edge of the huge mall parking lot. Trapped inside, she felt as if they'd gone miles.

"I don't remember hearing about any sale." The driver was skeptical. He was an older man with a full beard and a baseball cap pulled down low over his brow. "How do we know you weren't trying to steal a lawn mower?"

"I'm no thief," Nancy repeated firmly. The driver just stared at her.

"Do you know Frank Wexler?" Nancy asked. "He works for mall security here. He'll vouch for me."

The driver shook his head but finally relented. "I'm going to take your word for it, though I have my doubts. I know Frank, and I intend to ask him about you, Nancy Drew, when I have the time." His partner fished a piece of paper out of the pocket of his T-shirt and pulled a pencil from behind his ear. He jotted down Nancy's name.

"When you ask him, you'll see that I'm telling the truth," Nancy said.

"Well, whether you are or not, you're just lucky we heard you—and that you don't look like a person who'd rip off lawn mowers." The driver turned to his partner. "Close it up, Bob. Let's get rolling."

The two men closed up the truck and got back into the cab, then roared off.

Nancy stood by herself in the empty parking lot. Though she faced the long walk back to the mall, she was just grateful to be out in the fresh air and sunshine. Gradually her head cleared, and she realized that she was carrying Lesley Richards's backpack. It reminded her that she still had a lot of investigating to do if she intended to break this case. And she had to—if only for Bess and George. If the culprit wasn't uncovered by Friday, Ms. Long wasn't going to let Bess and the other salesclerks appear in the Lynxette video. And if the thief turned out to be Mr. X, Nancy definitely wanted him exposed before George became romantically involved with him.

Nancy's thoughts were suddenly disturbed when a hot red sports car pulled into a parking space right in front of her. A young woman with dark glasses and cascades of long blond curls stepped out. Nancy did a double take when she saw what the woman was wearing. It was a sapphire blue Morrell jacket with a red needlepoint rose on the back, just like the one Lesley Richards had won in the raffle the day before. But hadn't Bess told her that no two Morrell jackets were alike? If that was the case, then this had to be Lesley's jacket, the one that was stolen by the mugger.

"Excuse me," Nancy said to the woman. "I adore your jacket. Could you tell me where you got it?"

"Oh—thank you. It's a Morrell." The woman seemed to be torn between being flattered and nervous. "But they're very hard to get these days."

"It's awfully nice." Nancy pretended not to know anything about the Morrell jacket craze. "Where did you get this one? I'd love to get one for myself."

"Well . . ." Nancy could tell the woman was weighing her answer very carefully. "I—uh—I bought mine secondhand."

"Really? Where?"

Again the young woman hesitated. "Well . . . I bought it right here—in the parking lot."

"In the parking lot?"

"Ah, yes—from a man who sells them out of his car."

Nancy struggled to keep her face neutral. "How can I find him?"

"I don't know his name," the woman said. "I heard about him from a friend of mine who also bought a jacket from him. I was just told to look for him over there near the light pole with the letter *W* on it."

"What kind of car does this man have?"

The woman crinkled her face up. "Ummm—I'm terrible when it comes to cars. It was pretty big."

"What color was it?"

"I don't know. A dark color, I think."

"Black?" Nancy prompted.

"Well, it could have been black," the woman said nervously. "Or maybe navy or dark green. I can't say for sure. It was hard to tell. You see, I bought the jacket last night."

"And the guy who sold it to you—what did he look like?"

The young woman flipped her hair over her shoulder and shrugged. "He's somewhere between thirty-five and forty, I'd say. Stocky but muscular. Sort of rough looking."

"Anything else you remember," Nancy urged. "I'd really like to get one of these jackets."

The woman studied Nancy's face, then answered reluctantly. "He did have a tattoo on the back of his hand. An anchor, I think. A blue anchor." The young woman looked at her watch. "You know, I really have to go now. Good luck with the jacket." Giving Nancy a little wave, she started briskly toward the mall entrance.

Nancy couldn't say for sure whether the young woman knew she had bought a stolen jacket or not, but at least she had given Nancy a solid lead.

Nancy looked down at Lesley Richards's backpack. Maybe it was time to talk to Lesley again, she thought. Nancy picked up her pace and headed for the mall.

Nancy finally found Lesley at the food court. Sitting at a table, digging into a mound of french fries, Lesley didn't look like the recent victim of a crime. She looked happy, content, almost relaxed. Nancy was glad to see she was alone.

"Lesley," Nancy said, taking the chair across from her, "I'm glad I found you. I have something that belongs to you." Nancy laid the black backpack on the table. "It is yours, isn't it?"

Lesley went pale. "Gee, I don't know. It does sort of look like mine. But maybe not."

"I think it *is* yours, Lesley. An old library card with your name on it is inside."

Lesley looked a little ill.

"Your pack was in the back of a truck, a truck that your boyfriend Craig had just been in. I can see that you're not comfortable with any of this. Why don't you just tell me what's going on?"

"What are you getting at?" Lesley sounded defensive. "You and that security guy, Frank what's-his-name, you keeping asking me the same questions. I was mugged. Period."

Nancy leaned across the table. "I know you're hiding something, Lesley."

Lesley scoffed. "What are you—a mind reader or something?"

"No," Nancy said coolly. "But I am pretty good at putting two and two together. Either Craig had something to do with the mugging—or he's involved in the jacket thefts." Nancy let her words hang in the air a moment. Her ploy worked. Lesley paled even more.

"Why would my own boyfriend mug me?"

"You tell me." Nancy paused a moment, then added, "Or should I tell you?" She kept her fingers crossed and her mouth shut, so Lesley could speak. She had no idea what motive Craig could have for any of this. But a heartbeat later it was clear Nancy had hit a nerve.

"We *had* to do it."

"Do what?"

"Stage the mugging. The mugging never really happened. I just said it did. That's why I didn't want to report it to the police. It was just a story I made up, so I could sell my jacket."

"Why would you sell your jacket? Everyone in the world is dying to have one."

Lesley avoided Nancy's eyes. "I need the money," she said.

"Really?" This was hard for Nancy to believe, since Lesley was from a wealthy family.

"I know what you're thinking, that I'm a rich kid and that I can have whatever I want. But that's not true, Nancy. I'm on an allowance, and I haven't been sticking to it. I went a little crazy with my credit card—well, *very* crazy, to be honest—and I'm trying to raise money to pay it off before my parents find out. I asked Craig to get rid of my backpack, so that it would look like a mugging."

Nancy studied Lesley's face and tried to decide how much of her story to believe.

Finally she said, "I don't mean to pry into your personal life, Lesley, but can I ask you something?"

"What?"

"Your relationship with Craig—why does it have to be such a big secret?"

The corners of Lesley's mouth drooped. "I told you yesterday at the video arcade. My father doesn't approve of Craig."

"Because your fathers are business rivals?"

"Basically, yes. But Craig isn't anything like his father. Craig is different, and I love him."

Nancy studied Lesley's face. The sorrow and love she saw there seemed real enough.

But what about Dan Schaffer? Nancy suddenly pictured his name circled in red in Lesley's address book. Did she love him, too?

She pulled the address book out of her pocket and laid it on the table, opening it to the page where Dan's name and number were written.

"I think this is yours, too," Nancy said gravely.

Lesley's eyes widened in panic. "How did you . . ." Without finishing the sentence she tore the book from Nancy's hand. Then she jumped up and raced out of the food court.

Chapter Nine

LESLEY!" Nancy shouted after her, but the slender girl quickly disappeared into the arcade. What in the world was she up to? Nancy was tempted to follow Lesley, but so far her behavior, puzzling as it was, didn't seem connected to the shoplifting. Dan Schaffer, though —he was another matter.

Nancy decided it was time to talk to Dan directly. She dumped the contents of Lesley's tray into the waste container and stacked the tray on a shelf nearby. Then she headed toward CD City, where Dan worked.

On the way across the central court, Nancy ran into Frank. His face lit up when he saw her. "Hey," he said. "I was hoping I'd see you today. Things get so crazy, I didn't know if I'd have the chance."

"Got a minute?" Nancy asked, smiling up at him.

"Just," Frank said ruefully. "My boss is so worked up over this Lynxette scene, I can't be gone long." He tapped her arm lightly. "So how's the investigation coming along?"

Nancy stopped gazing into his eyes and forced her mind back to business. "I'm making a little progress on the thefts," she reported, and started to tell him what she'd learned.

Frank reached out and brushed a strand of Nancy's red-gold hair off her cheek. Between thrashing around in the truck, and the wind in the parking lot, Nancy suddenly realized her hair must be a tangled mess. Frank didn't seem to mind.

"Whoops!" He drew back suddenly. "My boss is over by the arcade. I'd better get moving." He gave her one last grin as he backed away. "See you."

"Yeah, see you," murmured Nancy, turning reluctantly back toward CD City. It was a moment before she realized she hadn't told him about finding Lesley's backpack, or about her conversation with Lesley in the food court. "Oh, Frank!" she cried, but he had vanished into the crowd.

Just then Nancy heard her name being called from another direction. It was George, loaded down with shopping bags. A quick look proved her friend had hit all the mall's sports stores.

"Hi!" George said, casting an eye down at her bags. "Bet you can't guess what I've been up to."

Nancy chuckled. "Haven't a clue."

"Actually, I was killing time before the in-line freestyle competition at RinkWorld."

"So you were checking out sales—"

"And looking for Mr. X," George admitted. "You haven't seen him—"

Nancy shook her head. George's grin faded a little. "Hey, I'm headed for CD City," Nancy said. "Want to come?"

"Sure, why not?" George said.

In keeping with Fashion Week, CD City had been transformed into the mall's Lynxette headquarters. A lifesize cutout of Lynxette in her gold Morrell jacket stood at the front of the store. "Money Talks" was blasting from the store's numerous speakers as the video monitors that hung from the ceiling played Lynxette's video. A group of kids mobbed the Lynxette bin, checking out all her old CDs. Half the girls in the store were wearing Morrell jackets.

George checked her bags at the door, then headed off to browse through the CDs. Nancy went up to the cash register. A girl with long cornrowed hair had just sold Lynxette's first CD to a girl in an orange Morrell jacket with a peace sign on the back. "Excuse me," Nancy said. "Is Dan Schaffer here?"

The salesclerk shook her head. "Sorry.

Dan's off today. He'll be here tomorrow after four. Do you want to leave him a note?"

"No, thanks," Nancy said. Recalling how unfriendly Dan had been toward her, she figured he'd avoid her if he knew she was looking for him. "I'll stop by again tomorrow."

As Nancy went over to get George, something caught her eye on the video monitor hanging over the entrance. The Lynxette video had ended, and a picture of Mara Morrell wearing her red- and white-striped hat replaced it. A redheaded veejay wearing a neon pink Morrell jacket stepped in front of Mara's picture. "That was Lynxette doing 'Money Talks,' " the veejay said. "And speaking of Lynxette, have you gotten your Mara Morrell jacket yet? Well, if you haven't, you're too late. The *Chicago Tribune* reports today that the wildly popular Morrell jackets have become the number one favorite with shoplifters all across the state. But the River Heights Mall has the dubious distinction of having had the most Morrell jackets stolen to date.

"Designer Mara Morrell has said that she regrets that her creation has become the object of a mini-crime wave, but, she adds, this is the kind of publicity you just can't buy. If, as expected, Lynxette wears another Morrell jacket when she films her video later this week in River Heights, demand for Ms. Morrell's phenomenal jackets will skyrocket.

And so, presumably, will the shoplifting incidents. . . ."

Nancy frowned as the next video came on. The kind of publicity you just can't buy, she thought, mulling over the report she'd just seen. A shoplifting epidemic that fuels a craze for Morrell jackets . . . Maybe this is no accident, she thought.

George wandered over, two vintage sixties CDs in her hand. "What's up, Nan?" she asked. "You must be cooking up something. I can see the wheels turning."

"Do you have anything planned for tomorrow?"

"No, nothing crucial."

"How would you like to drive up to Chicago?"

The next morning Nancy and George paid a visit to the Chicago offices of Morrell Designs, Incorporated. As they sat in front of a red lip-shaped coffee table in the waiting room, Nancy counted seven fashion magazines with cover stories on either Mara or her jackets. A blowup of a clipping from the *Wall Street Journal* hung on the wall next to a potted ficus tree. Like the report that Nancy had seen on TV, the article discussed the publicity that Mara was getting for free thanks to the crime wave and estimated that if she were to pay for that kind of promotion, it would cost several million dollars. Of course, once again, this was circumstantial evidence, but it was certainly motive enough for Mara to sponsor a ring of shoplifters to steal her own jackets.

"Ms. Drew? Ms. Fayne?" the receptionist said from behind her desk. She was a pretty girl, with long dark hair and dangling earrings. "Ms. Morrell said she'll see you now." She pointed down a hallway. "Just go straight that way. Her office is on the left. You can't miss it."

"Thank you." Nancy and George wandered down a stark white hallway until they found Mara Morrell's office. Nancy knocked on the opaque glass in the door.

"Come in!" the familiar voice trilled.

Walking through the door, Nancy felt as if she'd stepped through Alice's looking glass. Mara Morrell was sitting cross-legged on the floor surrounded by dozens of design sketches. She was wearing a jade silk Japanese kimono with lace-up lumberjack boots and a bright red velvet bowtie. Her hair was meticulously arranged on top of her head in what looked like large ribbon-candy loops. A slash of dark red lipstick was the only makeup on her face. She was hunched over a Ouija board, both hands on the pointer, a cordless telephone trapped between her ear and her shoulder.

"I told you, Avi, I'm picking the colors right now. I promise you, we will be going into production very soon, and you are at the top of my list. As soon as the new jackets are ready, you'll be one of the first to get them. I swear. Ta-ta, sweetie!"

Mara switched off the phone and tossed it aside, giving her full attention to the Ouija board and ignoring Nancy and George.

"Ms. Morrell?" Nancy said. "I'm—"

"One second. I'm getting something here." The pointer started to move across the board. *"F . . . U . . . C . . . H . . . S . . . I . . . A!* Fuchsia!" She looked up at Nancy. "Isn't that terrific?"

Nancy bit the insides of her cheeks to keep from laughing. "If you say so."

"I know this looks crazy," Mara explained, "but this is how I pick colors. The Ouija board has never let me down. So, what can I do for you?" Mara peered at Nancy over the bright red frames of her half-glasses. "Haven't I seen you somewhere before?" She looked at George. "You, too, sweetheart."

"My name is Nancy Drew, and this is George Fayne. We were at your fashion show at the River Heights Mall." Mara nodded distractedly. Nancy went on. "I'm investigating the shoplifting problem there, and I wanted to ask you a few ques—"

The phone rang. "Hang on," Mara said, putting the phone to her ear. "Hel-lo-o! Oh, Brian, it's you. How *are* you? . . . Well, yes, I know my jackets are all the rage in London. . . . No, I'm afraid I can't, not even for you, my love. . . . Why? Because I just don't have any. . . . No, not a single jacket. . . . Let me tell you, though. We're going into production very soon, and as soon as they're ready I will ship a gross out to you. Scout's honor . . . No, I won't forget. Bye-bye!"

She blipped off the phone and dropped it by her side as she returned to the Ouija board. "So," she said, focusing on the pointer again, "you were saying something about the River Heights Mall. It's such a shame how they've had all that shoplifting."

"Yes," Nancy said. "That's what I want to talk to you about. You see—"

"Hang on! Hang on!" The pointer was on the move. *"C . . . H . . . A . . . R . . . T . . . R . . . E . . . U . . . S . . . E!* Chartreuse! Isn't that genius?"

Nancy looked out of the corner of her eye at George. George was standing with her hands in her pockets, studying the ceiling. The corners of her mouth were working. Any minute she was going to crack up. Nancy forced herself to be serious. She coughed into her fist. "I wanted to ask you about the shoplifting problem—"

The phone rang again. Mara shrugged apologetically. "This is my private line for extra special customers. I *have* to take these calls, or else I'm dead in the water."

She put the phone to her ear. "Hello? . . . Oh, Jean-Claude, how have you been? . . . Great! Hold on one secundo." Her eyes shot open. "This is ultra!" she said to Nancy. "Jean-Claude calling from Paris. I *have* to take this one. I do want to talk to you, though. Why don't you fix yourselves a cup of coffee or tea or something? The kitchenette is down the hall."

Mara Morrell went back to her call from Paris, and Nancy felt more than a little put out, doubting that the designer would ever get off the phone long enough to answer a single question.

"I know, Jean-Claude, I know Paris is screaming for my jackets, but what can I do? I just don't have any to give you. . . . Of course, we're doing the best we can on this end. *Haute couture* is not built in a day, you know." Mara laughed her trilling laugh.

"This could take a while," George whispered.

Nancy nodded, and she and George went to look for the kitchenette. The coffee pot turned out to be empty, and they couldn't find teabags anywhere.

"I thought I saw a soda and juice machine in the hallway near the receptionist," George said, fishing in her knapsack for change. "Let's get something there."

Nancy shook her head. "I'd better wait here, in case Ms. Morrell's off the phone sooner rather than later."

"Fat chance!" George laughed. "I'll be back."

They went out into the hallway. George turned right outside the kitchenette. Nancy headed back toward Mara's office to be within earshot when the designer's call was done.

Nancy quickly noticed that Mara's offices were much larger than she'd thought and that there were more rooms in back. Her curiosity got the better of her, and she started to wander down the hallway, hoping to see some Mara Morrell designs in the making.

She came upon a room where everything was white, including the desk and chair. A drafting board was set up by a window that looked out on Lake Michigan. Sheets of paper littered the floor. Nancy figured that this must be where Mara created her designs. She was tempted to sneak in to see what Mara was working on.

Instead, hearing voices from farther down the hall, Nancy decided to follow them, eager to see what the rest of Mara's staff did. But the voices disappeared before she could find anyone. Nancy kept looking, anyway, going to the end of the hall to a big storeroom. Over by a freight elevator, she saw several long racks full of clothes covered with sheets of plastic.

Again Nancy's curiosity got the better of her. She couldn't wait to see what the new Mara Morrell fashions for next season would be and went over to take a peek.

But when she lifted the plastic sheet and looked underneath, she couldn't believe what she saw. There were dozens—no hundreds!—of the infamous Mara Morrell jackets, with a wide variety of patches on the back. Nancy checked the other racks, and it was the same thing, satiny jackets by the score. And after she'd just heard Mara tell three of her best customers that she didn't have any in stock!

George has to see this, Nancy thought. She backed away from the rack and started for the door. Suddenly an arm clamped down hard on her shoulder.

A hoarse voice growled in her ear, "What do you think you're doing here?"

Chapter Ten

"Let me go!" Nancy demanded, trying to turn around and squirm away. But the man didn't listen, tightening his grip instead.

He left her no choice. Nancy grabbed the man's forearm and bent forward, flipping him over her back and onto the floor with a judo throw. He landed hard.

"Oooowww!" he howled, covering his head. "Stop! Don't hurt me!"

Nancy propped her fists on her hips and glared at him. The man was overweight, with a round face and a shock of black hair that stuck out in all directions.

Mara Morrell and George ran into the back room, Mara's heavy lumberjack boots making a racket.

"What's going on?" the designer demanded.

The man on the floor pointed up at Nancy.

"I caught her in here trying to steal the jackets, and she attacked me."

"I was not trying to steal anything," Nancy objected hotly. "And he was the one who attacked me. He tried to choke me. I told him to let go, but he wouldn't listen."

Mara helped the man to his feet. "It's okay, Jimmy. She's here to see me. She's not a thief."

"I was just doing what you told me to do, Mara. Guard the jackets with my life—isn't that what you said?"

"Don't worry about it, Jimmy. It was just a misunderstanding." Mara brushed the man off and straightened his shirt collar. "This is my cousin Jimmy," she explained to Nancy. "He works for me."

"I see," Nancy said. She was still a little angry about being attacked from behind, but she could see that Jimmy was just doing what Mara had told him to do. To be honest it was partly her fault—she had been snooping.

George came up to Nancy and put an arm around her shoulders. "Are you okay?" she asked.

Nancy nodded. "Yes, I'm fine."

Jimmy climbed to his feet and looked down at the ground. "I'm sorry," he said to Nancy.

"And I apologize for tossing you." Nancy could see that he was embarrassed, and she felt sorry for him now.

Nancy then turned to the designer, more determined than ever to get some answers.

"Mara, I just heard you tell three people on the phone that you don't have any jackets. What are these then?" Nancy pointed to the racks of Morrell jackets. "Is this some kind of elaborate scheme you've put together to make your product scarce and to inflate prices?"

"My dear, my dear," Mara said, waving her hands, "you just don't understand how the fashion industry works. You have to make the public *want* your product, and the best way to do that is to make your product seem very precious and hard to get. That's why I'm telling everyone I don't have any. I want people to be absolutely crazy for them once I release the new batch."

"But that's unethical," George said.

Mara shrugged. "Maybe, but it's done all the time in the fashion industry. It's just the way the business is." She checked herself in a nearby mirror and fluffed her hairdo.

"But how far would you go to create a demand for your jackets, Mara?" Nancy pressed. "Would you arrange to have them stolen by the dozen to get 'the kind of publicity you just can't buy'?"

Mara wheeled around, horror registering across her face. It was the first genuine emotion Nancy had seen from her. "You're not the first person to insinuate that I'm behind the shoplifting, but I can tell you right now, Nancy, I have had absolutely nothing to do with that, and I never would. My father is a police officer, and I respect the law. Yes, I'm benefiting from the crime wave, but I am not happy that it's happening this way."

Mara was so uncharacteristically serious when she said this, Nancy couldn't help but believe she was telling the truth. "Then let me ask you this," Nancy said. "Can you think of anyone else who might benefit from all this publicity that the shoplifting has caused?"

"Well . . ." Mara rolled her eyes as she thought about it. "The stores that sell the jackets would benefit eventually. They're taking losses now, but when the new jackets arrive, kids will flock to the stores to buy them before they're stolen."

"Anyone else?" Nancy prodded.

"Well, to be brutally honest," Mara said, "Lynxette is probably getting something from this."

Nancy and George were totally baffled. "Lynxette?" Nancy said. "How would she benefit?"

"Truth is, her last CD almost bombed," Mara said. "The big hit single from it, 'Money Talks,' was at the bottom of the charts until the shoplifting hit the news. Then everybody wanted to see the video, so they could get a look at my jackets and find out what all the fuss was about. That's when people started paying attention to the song."

"Interesting," Nancy said.

"Not that the song is bad, but in the music biz, as in mine, quality's not enough to get the public's attention. You need a gimmick, a publicity stunt, something to turn people's heads. For Lynxette, it was my jackets. I mean, why do you think she's filming a second video with models wearing Morrell jackets? She knows a good thing, and she's going to ride this trend for all it's worth."

"Do you know Lynxette well?" Nancy asked. "It doesn't sound as though you two get along."

Mara threw her hands up and let out a hoot. "How can I dislike someone I hardly know? I have met her, yes, but she's always surrounded by an army of bodyguards and reporters and record execs and publicity agents. It's impossible to get close to her, and no one gets more than a minute of her time. And from what I hear, that's the way she likes it."

"Excuse me, Ms. Morrell?" The receptionist walked in and handed Mara a pink message slip.

While Mara read it, Nancy added this bit of information about Lynxette to what she already knew. It was hard to believe that someone as rich and famous as Lynxette would stoop to stealing jackets, but if it was a way for her to stay in the public eye, Nancy couldn't rule it out as a motive.

"Listen, Nancy," Mara said, "I really hate to cut you short, but I am *so* busy today. I want to help you with your investigation—I really do—so if there's anything I can do, call me." She held up the cordless phone, which was ringing again. "As you can see, I'm easier to talk to by phone than in person." She answered the phone. "Hello? . . . Oh, Dante! How are you? Can you hang on one moment?"

She put her hand over the phone. "Jimmy?" she called to her cousin. "One of Lynxette's assistants is downstairs in the parking garage. He wants the jackets that Lynxette and her models will be wearing for the new video."

Jimmy looked puzzled. "I thought they didn't need those jackets until Friday."

Mara shrugged. "You know Lynxette. She changes her schedule whenever it suits her. They're going to be filming at the River Heights Mall this afternoon."

This afternoon! Nancy thought in a panic. If she didn't catch the thief before then, Ms. Long might not let Bess and the other girls appear in the video. How in the world could she solve this case in just a few hours?

George sighed. "This doesn't look good," she said under her breath.

Mara pulled back the plastic sheet from the nearest clothes rack and separated the hanging jackets into two groups. "Jimmy, take this bunch down to Lynxette's assistant, then make sure the rest of them get to Wicked in River Heights today. Take the van and drive them there yourself. Ms. Long has been so good to us, I promised to get her a dozen more jackets. Have you got that, Jimmy?"

Jimmy nodded as he went over to the rack. "These are for Lynxette," he said, "and these are for Ms. Long at Wicked. I've got it."

"Go down now with Lynxette's jackets. Her assistant is waiting for you by the elevators. He's in a big hurry, of course."

"Lynxette's people always are," Jimmy said wearily as he pressed the button for the freight elevator.

"Hello, Dante? I'm back," Mara said into the phone, wandering back toward her office as she talked.

Nancy could see that she wasn't going to get any more of Mara's time, so she and George went back to the waiting room and showed themselves out, thanking the receptionist before they left. They took the elevator down to the parking garage where Nancy had left her blue Mustang.

The elevator dinged when it reached the parking garage. The girls stepped out and headed for Nancy's car. Straight ahead, at the other end of the garage, Nancy noticed Jimmy loading jackets into the trunk of a car. She still felt bad about their tussle, so she decided to go over and let him know that there were no hard feelings.

She handed George her car keys. "I'll meet you in the car. I want to talk to Jimmy for a minute."

"Okay," George said. "But could you make it fast? I'd really like to get back to the mall, so we can see Lynxette and maybe find Mr. X."

Nancy understood how George felt, and she had her own reasons for wanting to find him. What had he been doing in the truck the other day? Nancy wondered again if he was involved with the shoplifting. "I'll be quick," she said.

It was a long walk to the other end of the parking garage. Nancy's heels clicked out a beat on the concrete floor. The car Jimmy was loading jackets into was a black stretch limousine with dark tinted windows. She wondered if Lynxette was inside. Maybe she'd get her autograph.

Jimmy closed the trunk and went to the driver's side window, bending down to talk to the driver. This had to be Lynxette's assistant, Nancy thought. She couldn't see his face, though, because of the heavily tinted windshield.

"You're all set," Jimmy said to Lynxette's assistant. "They're all in the trunk."

"Thanks a lot, Jimmy." The engine started up with a roar. A hand emerged from the window to shake Jimmy's. As Nancy moved closer, she noticed something on the back of the assistant's hand. A tattoo. It looked like—an anchor, a blue anchor!

The hand slipped back inside the window, and suddenly the car lurched forward, tires squealing. Nancy's eyes shot open. She was right in its path! It was going to run her down!

Chapter Eleven

NANCY!" George's scream cut the silence of the garage.

For the barest instant, Nancy froze to the spot. The limousine was hurtling toward her, full speed.

Then she dove to the side, landing hard on the cold cement floor of the garage but rolling clear of the car.

The brakes screeched, and the driver's power window slid down. The man behind the wheel scowled at her. He was beefy, with a thick neck and dark slicked-back hair. He was also wearing dark glasses. "You all right?" he snapped.

"No thanks to you." Nancy got to her feet and worked her ankles and wrists. Her hand was bruised slightly from the concrete, but though she was sore, nothing seemed broken.

"Watch where you're going next time," he said. The window slid up, and the car sped toward the exit with tires squealing.

"Nancy! Are you hurt?" George yelled as she pounded across the parking garage toward her.

"I'm fine," Nancy answered as George came up and retrieved Nancy's bag from a corner, where it had landed. Nancy thanked her. "Now, where's Jimmy?" she asked as she brushed off her jacket.

"Over there." George pointed to a white van, a good fifty feet away, backing out of a parking spot. Painted on the door was Mara Morrell's double *M* logo, and Jimmy was behind the wheel.

"He must be on his way to River Heights with that shipment of jackets for Wicked," Nancy said.

"Jimmy," she called out, eager to ask him about the man with the tattoo. But Jimmy apparently didn't hear. The van just continued toward the exit. "Great—" Nancy muttered sarcastically. She'd found the man with the anchor tattoo on his hand, but how he fit into the shoplifting spree was a complete mystery. All he'd done so far was drive Lynxette's limo and sell a jacket to a woman in a parking lot. But maybe, she thought, he had organized the shoplifters. He was certainly connected to the jackets in some way. Or maybe he took orders from someone higher up—someone like Lynxette.

"George, I think we should follow that limo," Nancy said, starting for her car.

"Shouldn't we go to the mall first, to be sure nothing happens to that shipment of jackets?" George said, hopping into the passenger seat of Nancy's blue Mustang and buckling her seatbelt.

As Nancy peeled out of the parking space and up the exit ramp, she told George what she was thinking. It was probably no coincidence that Lynxette had chosen the mall with the highest number of Morrell jacket thefts as the place to film her new video. And she had a bad feeling that the shoplifter—whoever it was—would take advantage of all the confusion caused by Lynxette's appearance to top off this crime spree with something spectacular.

"We'll check out Lynxette first and go back to River Heights later."

But as they pulled out into the busy Chicago street, the stretch limo was nowhere to be seen. Nancy scolded herself for not acting quickly enough, but there was nothing to be done. The limousine was gone. After a few minutes Nancy headed toward River Heights.

Two hours later Nancy and George were riding the crowded escalator up to Wicked. The panoramic view from the escalator showed just how crazy Fashion Week was turning out to be. The lower level was swarming with people—people window-shopping, people waiting in line for lunch at the food court, people hanging out around the fountain —all of them killing time until Lynxette arrived. As she neared the top of the escalator, the scene below reminded Nancy of an ant farm—except that every third ant was wearing a colorful Morrell jacket.

"I'm not sure I follow your reasoning, Nan," George said. "Why do you think the thief will go back to Wicked?"

"If Jimmy told the guy with the blue anchor tattoo on his hand that he's delivering a dozen jackets to Ms. Long, and if the guy is the shoplifter, he'll target the store for sure," Nancy explained. "No other store in River Heights will have that many Morrell jackets."

George nodded. "I see what you're saying. You're probably right."

When the girls reached the upper level, the scene outside Wicked was insane. A gang of technicians was preparing the runway for the shooting of Lynxette's video. A rowdy group of reporters and photographers were noisily jockeying for places in front. Camera operators were carefully setting up equipment, loading film cartridges, and cleaning lenses. At least twenty girls in Morrell jackets were lined up outside Wicked, waiting to be transformed into Lynxette look-alikes by the three hair stylists and three makeup artists who were on duty at the makeshift dressing room that had been hastily set up at one end of the runway. An impatient crowd of die-hard Lynxette fans were milling around the area, singing their idol's songs in loud, boisterous voices.

As Nancy worked her way toward Wicked, she could see Bess and the other salesclerks in their black pageboy wigs, awaiting the big moment when Lynxette would arrive. As Nancy got closer, she could see that something wasn't right, though. Bess looked as if she was on the verge of tears. In fact, all the girls did. Ms. Long looked stern and determined.

"Bess, what's wrong?" Nancy asked.

Ms. Long answered before Bess could say a word. "What's wrong? I'll tell you what's wrong. We received a dozen jackets from Mara Morrell's studio less than half an hour ago, *and now they're gone!* The thief has struck again!"

Nancy and George gasped in unison. "That's unbelievable," Nancy said. "We saw the van leave Chicago and head straight here. Who knew they were coming?"

"Me. And my staff." Ms. Long's lips tightened. "No one else."

"Now we can't be in the video!" Bess cried.

"I'm sorry, but I have to put my foot down, girls," Ms. Long declared. "I can't rule out the possibility that one of you may be involved."

The girls all protested loudly.

Ms. Long lifted her hand for silence. "I'm sorry, but I want you all together until security talks to you. . . ."

"But—"

"No buts, Bess. That's the way it has to be."

"Isn't there something we can do to change your mind, Ms. Long?" Nancy asked. She felt terrible for Bess and the other girls. Getting to be in a rock video was a once-in-a-lifetime opportunity.

Ms. Long shook her head. "I'm sorry, Nancy. I'm sure you mean well, but I just can't take a chance. If you do catch the thief before the taping, the girls can be in the video."

Nancy scanned the faces of all the girls. She felt sure none of them was involved with the crime. "What time do they start filming?" she asked.

"Three-thirty," Bess said.

Nancy took a deep breath. She didn't have a whole lot of time, but she was willing to give it her best shot.

"Okay," Nancy said to Ms. Long as she headed out of the store, "I'll do what I can. But I can't make any promises."

Nancy was determined, but her heart sank as soon as she saw the sea of people jamming the upper level of the mall. How in the world was she going to find a thief in that mob? Would the thief even be in the mall still? All she could do was try—and hope the thief had hung around to steal the jackets the extras in the video were wearing. She glanced at her wristwatch. She had less than three hours.

Just then George grabbed Nancy by the arm. She was pale and out of breath. "I found him," she gasped.

"Who?" Nancy asked. "The man with the blue tattoo?"

"No! Mr. X!"

George dragged Nancy out into the hall and made her look toward the escalators nearest Wicked. Mr. X was standing at the railing in his long tweed overcoat. When he noticed them his expression darkened. He started to work his way through the crowd toward them.

Mr. X moved quickly, cutting through the throng of shoppers. Nancy suddenly realized he was focused on her, not George, and he was charging toward her like a bull who had just seen red!

Chapter Twelve

FISTS CLENCHED by his side, Mr. X stopped just inches from Nancy. "You're Nancy Drew, aren't you?" He glared down at her, his dark eyes furious.

"Why, yes—I am," Nancy said cautiously.

"Well, where do you get off accusing me of shoplifting?"

Nancy was totally shocked. "I never accused you of anything," she said. "I don't even know you." Even though he was one of her prime suspects, only George and Frank knew it.

"Frank Wexler from mall security has been trailing me all day. When I finally turned on him, he admitted I was suspected of shoplifting. I denied it, of course. I let him check my pockets, the trunk of my car, everything." Mr. X shook his head, then went on angrily. "He eventually apologized, but I demanded to know who had fingered me. He wouldn't say, but later I did overhear some girl saying Nancy Drew was snooping around the mall accusing people of all sorts of crimes. She gave me a pretty good description of you and said that you'd been hanging out around Wicked."

Lesley, Nancy thought, then defended herself out loud. "I haven't *accused* anyone of anything."

Suddenly Nancy remembered George. Out of the corner of her eye, Nancy could see her friend blushing deeply. Obviously George never expected that her first meeting with Mr. X would be like this. But the young man was so angry, he didn't seem to notice George at all, which was even worse. Nancy had to do something, fast.

First, though, she needed answers to a few more questions. Frank might have cleared the man because he didn't find evidence on him, but that didn't mean he wasn't guilty. Could Mr. X be tied in with the man with the tattoo? For George's sake Nancy softened her approach. "I'm sorry you were hassled," she said, trying to calm him down. "I really didn't want this to happen, but we did see you hanging around the mall, and you didn't seem to be doing any shopping."

"Of course, I wasn't shopping," Mr. X said indignantly, and fished a notepad and handheld tape recorder out of one of his coat pockets. He flapped them under Nancy's nose. "I'm here doing research for a term paper."

"A term paper?"

"Yes. I'm an architecture student at Westmoor University, and I'm doing a term paper on shopping mall design. That's why I've been spending all day here. The bigger stores all gave me free access to come and go as I pleased."

Ah-ha, Nancy thought, that's why he disappeared when she and George followed him into Davidson's Department Store. He knew his way around, and must have had access to the back rooms.

"I happened to see you getting into the back of a truck parked at Davidson's loading dock yesterday," Nancy said. "Was that part of your research?"

"Of course. I was measuring the dimensions of the trailer, trying to figure out how I could improve the design of the loading dock.

"I see," Nancy said.

"Unfortunately," Mr. X went on more slowly, "I forgot to tell security what I was up to." He had finally calmed down. "So it's partly my fault, I guess." He rumpled his hair and looked a little sheepish. "By the way, I'm Darryl Blake." He extended his hand and shook Nancy's.

It was the perfect opportunity for Nancy to introduce him to George, who was slowly inching away from them.

"And, Darryl," Nancy said quickly, "I'd like you to meet my friend—"

"Bess Marvin," Bess said, squeezing in between Nancy and George. "I couldn't help but overhear you say you're not the shoplifter, Darryl. Well, if you're not, why do you always wear that baggy overcoat? That looks like a shoplifter's tool if I ever saw one."

Darryl narrowed his eyes. "I happen to love this coat. I wear it all the time."

"Oh, really?" Bess said, crossing her arms.

Bess could be awfully stubborn, and Nancy knew she was desperate to find the thief—any thief—so that she could be in the video. But Nancy had to cut off Bess before she completely ruined George's chances for getting to know Darryl Blake.

"George," Nancy said before Bess could get another word in, "*you* know a lot of people at Westmoor. Maybe you and Darryl have some friends in common."

Suddenly Darryl's eyes widened. It was as if he had noticed George for the first time. If he was still angry, the anger instantly melted away as his eyes met George's. A gorgeous smile brightened his face. "I'm sorry," he said to George, "I didn't catch your name."

"It's George. George Fayne." George was trying to suppress a grin and wasn't doing a very good job of it.

"George," he repeated. "What an interesting name. I'd love to hear who you know at Westmoor. Would you like to go down to the food court and have a soda?"

George smiled and quickly nodded her head.

"I'll see you back here later," George said to Nancy. "And thanks," she whispered in Nancy's ear.

As George and Darryl walked off and disappeared into the crowd, Nancy noticed Dan Schaffer coming off the escalator. He was heading for Wicked, but as soon as he spotted Nancy standing in front of the store, his face fell. He picked up his pace and walked right by, going into the crowd gathered around the runway.

"There's Dan," Bess said, happy to see him. "I wonder where he's going."

"What's that in his hands?" Nancy asked, squinting to try to make it out.

"Hey!" Bess said in surprise. "It looks like a copper-colored Morrell jacket."

"I think you're right," Nancy said. "But where could he have gotten it? I thought there were none left in River Heights."

Bess bit her bottom lip. "You don't think he . . . No . . . He can't be the thief. Not Dan. Can he, Nancy?"

Nancy squeezed Bess's shoulders. "I don't know, but I'm going to find out. You go back to work." Nancy tore off after Dan, but the crowd slowed her down.

Oh, no! she thought, hopping up and down to see over the heads of the people in front of her. I'm going to lose him.

Dan was all the way on the other side of the runway now, but Nancy wasn't giving up. She worked her way to the runway and climbed up onto it. If she cut across, she might be able to catch up with him.

She tore off across the runway, slipping past the technicians who were busy taking down the temporary guardrail so that they could replace it with a painted backdrop for Lynx-ette's video.

If only she were wearing better shoes for running, Nancy thought, and not the heels she'd worn for her meeting with Mara Morrell that morning.

The clearest path along the runway was the side closest to the edge. As Nancy picked up her pace she was very aware that on her right there was nothing but open space dropping off to the lower level.

Undaunted, Nancy hurried down the run-way, determined to get to Dan Schaffer to find out how and where he had gotten that jacket. Nancy was almost at the end of the runway when one of the photographers stepped onto the platform and into Nancy's path. With a camera up to his eye, he didn't see Nancy. She veered around him to avoid a collision.

"Watch out!" she yelled, her heel suddenly turning. Nancy found herself tottering on the edge of the runway. She gasped and her heart leaped into her throat.

Directly below her was the central court and

the fountain, a thirty-foot drop straight down. She tried to catch herself by flailing her arms. She stumbled and was perched right on the brink, teetering. The pool below, she knew, was much too shallow to break her fall safely.

Chapter Thirteen

As Nancy lost her balance and was ready to plunge forward, someone grabbed her arm and yanked her back. Nancy found herself sagging against a muscular chest.

When she turned around and saw who it was, she gasped. Dan!

"Are you all right?" Dan kept a tight hold on her and helped her down from the runway. The video crew hovered around a moment, then turned back to their work shaking their heads. Looking down, Nancy saw the copper-colored Morrell jacket on the floor where Dan had dropped it.

It took a second for Nancy to find her voice. "I'm okay," she finally said, and swallowed hard. "You saved my life." When she looked up, Dan instantly averted his gaze.

Nancy stepped back, regaining her composure. Without another word, Dan picked up the jacket and started to walk away.

"Wait," Nancy said.

He froze, facing away from her.

"Let's get out of the crowd," she said. She grabbed his sleeve and steered him toward Bookworms. They stopped near the store entrance.

"I'm really in a hurry," Dan said. "I can't talk now—"

"Why are you so uncomfortable whenever I'm around?" Nancy asked, cutting him off. "Every time you see me, you go the other way."

Dan hung his head and sighed. "Don't you remember me?"

"What do you mean?" Nancy asked. "We just met a couple of days ago."

He seemed genuinely surprised. "You mean you *don't* remember?"

"Remember what?"

Dan sighed again. "Back when I was in sixth grade, I was your paperboy. I was the one who threw your paper through the window on your porch."

It took Nancy a moment to recall the broken window. "You're right. Someone did break the window once, years ago."

"That was me. I did it and never owned up to it. I quit my route that very day, and I never told a soul what I had done. I sort of figured your dad and you knew it was me."

So *that's* why he'd been acting weird. Nancy was tempted to laugh, but Dan was obviously upset. "Dan, I'm sure my dad forgot about that window ages ago. Anyway, it's all water under the bridge now."

"Are you sure?" Dan's face brightened.

"Absolutely, but I've got to ask you something."

Panic crossed Dan's face again. "What?"

Nancy pointed to the Morrell jacket. "What are you doing with that? And why did I find your name and phone number in Lesley Richards's address book?"

Dan looked first to the right then to the left. He dropped his voice. "I shouldn't tell you," he said, and heaved a sigh. "Just keep quiet about it. You see—I've been privately tutoring Lesley in math, so that she won't flunk out. But she doesn't want anyone to know."

"I see." Nancy nodded. So that explained why Lesley was so embarrassed when Nancy confronted her with Dan's name in her address book. She didn't want anyone to know that she needed tutoring.

Nancy pointed to the jacket again. "But what about this, Dan?"

Dan looked puzzled. "The jacket?" Then a horrified expression crossed his face. "You think I ripped it off?"

"I don't know what to think. I know they haven't been available here for days."

"I got this one at the Farmdale Mall," Dan

said proudly. "I've been saving up for it. For Bess."

"This jacket is for Bess?"

"Who else? I was a little embarrassed that I had to borrow gas money from Bess to get to Farmdale, but I'll pay her back." Dan held up the jacket to show Nancy the patch on the back. It was a needlepoint picture of a chocolate kiss.

"She'll love it," Nancy said, relieved that Dan wasn't the shoplifter and pleased that Bess had a boyfriend who cared enough to buy her something she really wanted.

She checked her watch. It was getting closer to the time that Lynxette was scheduled to arrive, and the crowds were getting bigger. If Nancy was going to find the shoplifter in time for Ms. Long to let her sales staff appear in the video, she had to get moving. Now that she had crossed Dan and Mr. X from her list of suspects, she had only two more people to check out, the guy with the blue anchor tattoo and Craig Jordan.

Craig had helped Lesley arrange her bogus mugging so she could sell her sapphire blue Morrell jacket, Nancy reasoned, and it was the man with the blue tattoo who had sold that jacket to the young woman in the parking lot, so it seemed possible Craig knew something about all this.

Nancy said goodbye to Dan and raced over to the mall maintenance department, where

Craig worked. It was tucked down a long deserted hallway near the automotive department of Davidson's. The sudden quiet combined with the stark cinder-block walls of the hallway made Nancy feel as if she'd just stepped into a tomb.

Her heels clicked ominously on the cement floors. The hallway ended in a *T*. To the left was another long hallway lined with closed doors. The hallway to the right was shorter, and she could see light spilling out of an open doorway. She decided to check out that room first, wondering how Craig would react when she confronted him with her suspicions.

But when she peeked into the room, instead of Craig, she found a stocky, snowy-haired man sitting at a metal desk, filling out forms. He was wearing a bottle green cardigan sweater over a khaki work shirt and slacks. The plaque on his desk said Bernie Olsen, Director of Maintenance.

"Excuse me," Nancy said politely.

The man didn't raise his eyes from his work.

"Excuse me," she repeated a little louder.

There was still no reaction.

"Excuse me!" she nearly shouted.

"What?" The man whipped up his head and fiddled with something in his ears. It took Nancy a second to realize that he was turning up the volume on his hearing aids. "Can I help you?" he asked in a hoarse but kindly voice.

"I'm looking for Craig Jordan," she said.

"I'm afraid Craig doesn't work here anymore," Mr. Olsen said, putting down his pen. "He quit this morning."

"He quit?" Nancy was startled. "Why?"

The man shrugged. "Said he didn't need the money anymore. Just came in and said he was quitting, effective immediately. I didn't question him about it. His father's one of the bigwigs around here, you know."

"Yes, I know." Nancy also knew that Mr. Jordan wanted his son to work for his spending money.

"Mr. Olsen, my name is Nancy Drew—"

"Oh, you're the one who's working on this shoplifting problem. Frank Wexler told me all about you. Having any luck?"

Nancy smiled. She couldn't help being pleased at the thought of Frank talking about her. "Well, I'm doing the best I can. But maybe you can help me."

"Sure. I will if I can." Mr. Olsen sat back in his swivel chair and put his feet up on the desk.

"Can you tell me when Craig started working for you?"

"Well, let's see." Mr. Olsen pulled out the bottom drawer of his desk and removed a file folder, tilting his head back so he could see through the bottom of his bifocals. "Hmmm . . . He started four weeks ago. Only here a month."

"Four weeks ago." Bess had said the shoplifting problem started four weeks ago, too,

Nancy thought. "And what exactly did Craig do in the maintenance department?" Nancy asked.

"Well, he was what we call a general helper, which is just a nice way of saying he cleaned up after the carpenters and electricians, picked up trash from the small stores, did odd jobs for them whenever they needed something done."

"Just the small stores? What about the big ones?"

"The big ones like Davidson's have their own maintenance people," Mr. Olsen said. "My people service the smaller stores as well as taking care of the public areas of the mall."

"Uh-huh. Did Craig have access to these smaller stores?"

"Well, yes, he did have a set of keys to all the back doors when he was on duty." Mr. Olsen suddenly frowned. "What are you getting at? Do you think he's done something wrong?"

"I really can't say, sir. I'm just collecting evidence right now." In fact, Nancy couldn't say for sure whether Craig was the thief or not. She now knew that as a maintenance worker he had opportunity, but did he have a motive? Unless he was trying to make some easy money—money that his strict father wouldn't give him—by selling the stolen jackets.

"Well, thanks for your time, Mr. Olsen," Nancy said as she started to leave. "I'll let you get back to work."

"Oh, Ms. Drew?"

Nancy turned back at the doorway. "Yes?"

"If you want to talk to Craig yourself, he said he'd be here in about a half hour to pick up his last paycheck. You're welcome to come back if you like."

"Thanks," she said.

"Anytime." He grinned and went back to his paperwork. Nancy noticed him turn down his hearing aids again.

Nancy headed back the way she'd come, wondering what she was going to do about Craig. If he was the thief—and she wasn't absolutely certain that he was—how was she going to flush him out? And could she do it in time for Bess to be in the Lynxette video?

Nancy was about to turn the corner and start down the long corridor that led back out to the mall when she heard footsteps coming from that direction. Stopping, she peered around the corner, being careful not to be seen. When she saw who it was, her heart nearly stopped. At the far end of the hall was the man who had almost run her over in Chicago that morning—the man with the tattoo. His expression was grim. He was wearing a black suit over a white T-shirt and carrying two stuffed, brown plastic garbage bags over his shoulders.

Full of Morrell jackets? she wondered instantly.

The man stepped closer and Nancy pulled back. After a moment she peeked around the corner again. This time she could definitely make out the tattoo on the man's hand. He continued to come closer, and Nancy quickly glanced around. Except for Mr. Olsen's office, there was nowhere to hide.

Just then the tattooed man stopped in front of a door and knocked. When it opened he went inside. The noise when it slammed echoed throughout the cold corridor.

Nancy hesitated for just a second. She knew she should go for help, try to find Frank. But she also knew she had little if no time to lose. Taking off her shoes, she tiptoed up to the door in her stocking feet. The cold cement sent a chill up her spine. Nancy pressed her ear against the metal surface of the door.

"I'm telling you, Craig, she was even snooping around Morrell's office."

Nancy gasped out loud, then clapped her hand over her mouth. Obviously, Craig and the guy with the tattoo were well acquainted.

"You mean that good-looking chick with the reddish hair?" Craig laughed harshly.

"Yeah," said the tattooed guy. "I figured she was snooping around to find out about the jackets."

"I know *all* about her," Craig said. "Her name's Nancy Drew, and she thinks she's some sort of detective. Soon enough she's going to snoop her way into some serious trouble."

"Well," the man's voice grew even more flat and menacing. "I'm not about to let some girl muck up our plan."

"Hey, Jake, no rough stuff," Craig said, his tone changing. "Stealing's one thing but—"

Jake snickered. "Getting scared, rich boy?" He laughed outright. "It's time you learned, kid. In a game like this, there's more than one way to make a killing."

Chapter Fourteen

NANCY'S FIRST IMPULSE was to bolt. Her heart was racing so fast she could hardly think straight. "Calm down," she murmured to herself, somewhat comforted by the sound of her own voice. She took a couple of deep breaths and began to ease back from the door.

Craig's next words riveted her to the spot. "How many do you have there, Jake?"

Curiosity made Nancy creep closer. She pressed her ear against the door and forgot about her fear. "Two dozen," the guy with the tattoo said. "These are the ones that were supposed to be used in the video today."

"So what are they going to use for the video? Won't Lynxette be angry?"

"Not to worry," Jake said. "There's got to be a thousand kids out there wearing Morrell jackets. I'm sure they can get plenty of volunteers from the crowd."

"No doubt about that," Craig said. "Hey, Jake, check this out." The rustling of plastic carried through the door. "I got these from the back room at Wicked. Morrell sent them down earlier today."

"Did you have a hard time getting them?"

"No harder than any of the other times. It's like taking candy from a baby when you've got the keys to the back door—and this."

Jake chuckled. "What's that gizmo?"

"It deactivates the security tags—all the smaller stores are using the same system."

"Not too smart," Jake remarked.

Craig went on. "All you need is a little diversion—like a blackout or a fire in a garbage can—to distract the staff."

"You're a regular prince of thieves, kid," Jake said. "You've really got it down to a science."

Craig was the thief. No doubt now. Nancy gritted her teeth. She couldn't stand their cocky attitude.

"So what're we going to do with three dozen jackets?" Jake asked. "I don't think I should sell these out in the parking lot. Cops are crawling all over the place trying to control the crowd. And at this point, I don't want to take any chances."

"Don't worry, Jake. I can sell them, no problem. Remember that lady who bought the blue jacket with the red rose patch on the back, the jacket that my girlfriend won?"

"Yeah?"

"Her name is Dawn Matthews, and she keeps sending her girlfriends to me. They all want Morrell jackets. I usually tell them to go find you in the parking lot, but I'm sure I can unload these on Dawn's friends in no time."

"Good thinking," Jake said. "Let's hit the food court. You can have whatever you want. On me."

Nancy heard their footsteps moving toward the door. She had to get out of there before they caught her eavesdropping. She raced to the end of the corridor and turned right toward Mr. Olsen's office again.

Behind her, Craig and Jake's door creaked open as Nancy made a mad dash for Mr. Olsen's office and ran in.

The startled head of maintenance looked up from his paperwork and quickly turned on his hearing aids. Nancy suddenly realized that Mr. Olsen's deafness probably kept him from hearing Craig and Jake's comings and goings. "Ms. Drew!" he said. "What's wrong?"

"Ah . . . I . . ." Nancy's heart was pounding.

"You're all out of breath," Mr. Olsen said. "You must've come back here for a reason."

Nancy peeked out into the hallway. It was empty, thank goodness. "Well, Mr. Olsen," she said, thinking fast, "I was, ah—I was wondering if you would do something for me."

He looked a bit puzzled. "I will if I can."

"Well, I was wondering if I could leave a note for Craig. You said he'd be coming back for his paycheck this afternoon. You could give it to him then."

A smile of relief broke out across Mr. Olsen's alarmed face. "Is that all? Why, of course, I'll give him a note. Do you need a piece of paper?"

"Yes, please."

He ripped a piece from the tablet on his desk and handed Nancy one of his pens. Nancy set the paper down on top of a file cabinet and wrote standing up.

> Dear Craig,
> I'm a good friend of Dawn

Nancy stopped to rack her brain. Oh, what did Craig say her last name was? Oh, yes!

> I'm a good friend of Dawn Matthews. She told me I could buy some jackets from you. I need at least a dozen, preferably two, but I need them today. Meet me at the loading dock behind Davidson's at three o'clock. I'll bring cash.

Nancy stopped and thought for a few moments, then finally she signed it, "Sincerely, Heather Harrison."

She folded the note in half, then in half again.

"I'll make sure he gets it," Mr. Olsen said, taking the note and his pen back. "And I promise not to peek," he added with a mischievous wink.

"Oh, please don't," Nancy said. "It's kind of personal."

"Not to worry," Mr. Olsen said, sticking the note in an envelope and licking the flap. He sealed it and wrote Craig's name on the front.

"Thank you, Mr. Olsen," Nancy said as she headed out again. " 'Bye."

Nancy knew she had to act fast. In less than an hour she had to catch Craig. She could use Frank's help, but there was no time.

As she jogged down the hall, it occurred to her that she'd better have a backup plan, in case something went wrong. If she knew exactly where Craig hid his stash of jackets, she could lead mall security to it. With all the craziness out in the mall, she knew security wouldn't get to it right away, though. Time was definitely a factor. She had to nab Jake and Craig before the filming of the Lynxette video began. Maybe the jackets were still in the room in which she had heard Craig and Jake talking.

Nancy went back to that room and slowly turned the knob to open the door a crack to make sure they weren't inside. The room was pitch-black. She opened the door a little wider, then reached in for the wall switch. The overhead fluorescent lights flickered on, revealing a large storeroom cluttered with gallons of cleaning solvents and floor wax, dozens of stacked cardboard boxes in all sizes, three electric floor buffers, and an array of mops and brooms that hung on hooks next to the electrical panel box. Sets of keys dangled from hooks on a small peg board nearby. Shoved into a corner with some spare trash cans was a collection of bulging garbage bags, just like the two that Jake had carried in.

Nancy closed the door behind her, then worked her way through the jam-packed room, stepping over boxes and floor buffers to get to the garbage bags. No one would ever suspect there was anything worth stealing in this mess, she thought. When she finally reached the bags, she stooped down and started to undo the twist tie on the nearest one. She wasn't surprised to find a collection of satiny colors inside.

The bag was full of Morrell jackets, each one with the same patch—a needlepoint portrait of Lynxette. The tag in the collar of the one on top—a silver jacket—said "Special Lynxette Edition." Nancy did a quick count. Fourteen, just one short of a complete set. These would fetch a very good price, Nancy thought, but they would also be easy to trace if Craig and Jake sold them. She'd have to keep this in mind in case her plan failed.

She closed the bag and replaced the twist tie as fast as she could. According to her watch it was a little after two-thirty. She had less than an hour to put this all together.

But as she stood up and started to step over a floor buffer, she suddenly heard something. She froze and listened, her heart thumping. Then she whipped her head up and saw the doorknob turning.

There was nowhere to hide. Nancy braced herself to spring past the intruder.

Then she saw who it was.

"Nancy! What are *you* doing here?" Lesley Richards stood in the doorway, wearing another Morrell jacket. This one was hot pink.

"I think I should be asking what *you're* doing here," Nancy said, trying to steady her voice.

"I'm looking for Craig, if you must know. But that's none of your business," Lesley huffed. She crossed her arms and turned her back on Nancy.

Suddenly Nancy saw the patch on the back of Lesley's new jacket. It was a needlepoint portrait of Lynxette, obviously from the set of stolen jackets in the bag Nancy had just opened. Nancy's heart sank. She had hoped Lesley wasn't involved in Craig's criminal activities, but this didn't look good.

"Lesley, that's a new jacket, isn't it?" Nancy asked. "Where did you get it?"

"If you must know, Craig gave it to me this morning," Lesley said. "I'm just trying it on."

"Do you know that it's stolen?" Nancy asked.

Lesley wheeled around to face Nancy. "It is not!" she snapped. "Craig *bought* it for me."

"Where did he buy it?" Nancy asked.

Lesley shrugged. "I don't know. Somewhere here at the mall. Wicked, probably."

"Probably not," Nancy countered. "There haven't been any Morrell jackets available here in days. Wicked was cleaned out this morning."

Lesley looked nervous all of a sudden. "Well, maybe he went to another mall. I don't know."

"That's possible. Maybe he did," Nancy conceded. "I guess he felt bad for you because you had to sell the sapphire blue one that you had won."

Lesley was *very* nervous now. "Yes—he did feel bad."

"Lesley, why don't you tell me what's going on?"

"All right, all right, I'll tell you, but I don't want you to make more of this than there is, okay? Remember when I told you that I sold my jacket because I needed the money to pay off my credit card bills?"

"Yes, I remember."

"I lied. I sold it to help Craig pay off *his* credit card bills. I was trying to help him out."

"Hold on," Nancy objected. "That makes no sense. Craig comes from a wealthy family. I'm sure his father would bail him out if he got into trouble with his credit cards."

Lesley gave a small, sarcastic laugh. "Craig's

father's a first-class tyrant. He insists that Craig pay all his own bills. Mr. Jordan is constantly lecturing Craig, telling him how he worked his way through college, then started his own business and made millions. He wants Craig to be just like him—but that's the last thing Craig wants."

Nancy frowned, skeptical about what she was hearing. "Hold on, Lesley. First you tell me Craig bought you this new jacket. Now you're telling me that he's in debt, and his father would never dream of helping him. This doesn't make any sense."

"Yes, it does!" Lesley insisted. "You're trying to paint Craig like a criminal. He's not. I knew you'd try to make more of this than there was." Lesley stepped closer to Nancy. "Craig's a good guy—a little mixed up, but who isn't?" She paused. "Don't you get it? I love him."

Nancy refused to back down. "Then explain it to me, Lesley. I want to understand."

"Craig told me he bought this jacket on time," Lesley said. "You know, store credit. He'll pay a little each week for the next month until it's paid off. He told me he intended to work overtime to do it. It's a big deal. He bought it because he cares for me. Don't you understand?"

Nancy ignored the plea in her voice and met her gaze steadily. "Overtime? That's what he told you? How does he plan to do that when he just quit his job?"

The color drained from Lesley's face. "What?"

"His boss just told me. He quit."

Lesley's chest was heaving as she glared at Nancy. "Liar!" she yelled, and burst into tears.

Nancy watched as Lesley covered her face with her hands and slid down the wall with her back against it. She clasped her knees to her chest, then lowered her face and wept.

Nancy felt terrible. It was clear that Lesley loved Craig, but he'd been lying to her all along.

"Everybody hates Craig," Lesley sobbed. "You, my friends, my parents, his father. You all want to think the worst of him, but he's not like that. He isn't." Lesley buried her face in her hands.

Nancy's heart was aching for her, but the truth was the truth, and Lesley had to face it. Nancy worked her way to the back of the room and picked up the garbage bag full of the Morrell jackets with the Lynxette patches. She opened it and pulled one out for Lesley to see. "I found these back here, Lesley, and this isn't the only bag. I also overheard Craig and his accomplice, some thug named Jake, discussing how they were going to sell these."

"No!" Lesley turned her back on Nancy, refusing to listen.

Nancy glanced at her watch. It was a quarter to three. Craig would be back in fifteen minutes to pick up his paycheck, and Mr. Olsen would give him the note she'd written. She had to get moving if she was going to catch Craig.

She closed the bag and quickly replaced the twist tie, tossing the bag back on the pile. Once again she started climbing over the buffers and boxes, watching her step as she worked her way to the door. "I'm sorry I had to tell you all this, Lesley—I really am—but it's better that you know now before Craig gets you involved in something that lands you into real trouble."

"I'm not the one in trouble here, Nancy Drew. You are." In a flash, Lesley sprang to her feet. She was lithe and small and beat Nancy to the door.

Nancy reached for the doorknob, but Lesley blocked it. Again Nancy grabbed for the knob. This time Lesley viciously kicked Nancy in the shin and in the next moment sprang out the door.

Chapter Fifteen

LESLEY'S KICK had caught Nancy off guard, with no time to avoid the blow. Now, as she stood bent over, catching her breath, Nancy realized that Lesley was getting away. Limping slightly, Nancy headed for the corridor.

"Lesley, stop!" Nancy shouted after her.

"No way," Lesley called over her shoulder. "I'm finding Craig and telling him about the lies you're spreading."

Tell Craig! That would blow everything. "Lesley, don't!" Nancy yelled.

She raced down the hall toward the double doors that led back to the mall, then pushed through them and into the thick of the crowd. After a few moments of searching she spotted Lesley's dark, spiky hair and the hot pink Morrell jacket, now tucked under Lesley's arm. Catching up to her, Nancy blocked her way. "Lesley," she panted. "You've got to listen. Craig's involved in something serious—"

"Get out of my way!" Lesley tried to shove past Nancy, refusing to look her in the eye.

Nancy had no time to waste arguing. She had to put her plan in action before Lesley found Craig and spilled the beans. "Oh, forget it!" she cried in disgust. She turned on her heel and pushed toward the escalator and got on.

She could hear Lesley's voice behind her. "What are you going to do?" Lesley yelled.

Nancy refused to stop. The whole upper level of the mall was teeming with Lynxette fans anxiously waiting for their idol to appear. Looking over toward the runway in front of Wicked, Nancy could see a rock band tuning up while the film crew adjusted the elaborate scaffold of lights they'd constructed. Dozens of girls in Morrell jackets and short black Lynxette wigs were waiting for the filming to start, even though it wasn't supposed to happen for another forty-five minutes. Bess must be tearing her hair out, Nancy thought. Lynxette herself was nowhere in sight, but a platoon of uniformed police officers circled the stage, standing shoulder to shoulder to keep the fans off the runway.

Nancy plowed still deeper into the crowd, hoping to lose Lesley in all the confusion. She moved quickly, slipping around the Lynxette fans and mall rats but not running because she might give her position away to Lesley. But as she got closer to the runway, the crowd grew thicker, and it was like moving through Jell-O. By the time Nancy reached Wicked, she was out of breath.

"Nancy!" Bess cried as Nancy finally made her way into the store. "Did you catch the thief?" Bess and the other sales clerks were still in costume, hoping that Nancy would save the day for them.

But Ms. Long was standing behind the cash register, arms folded. "Well, Nancy? Have you caught the thief?"

"Not yet, Ms. Long, but I plan to very soon," Nancy said. "I'm going to need a little help, though. Could I borrow Bess for about a half hour?"

"Me?" Bess squeaked.

"You do want to be in the video, don't you?" Nancy asked.

"Bess, you've *got* to!" the other girls urged.

Bess gulped. "Okay. What do I do?"

"You wouldn't happen to still have George's camera?" Nancy asked, hoping Bess forgot to return it as she did everything else.

"Yes. It's in my purse."

"Speaking of George, where is she?"

Bess shrugged. "She's gone off with Darryl Blake. They're somewhere in the crowd waiting for Lynxette."

Nancy pressed her lips together. She had been hoping George would be here, so she could send her to find Frank and let him know what the plan was. Secretly Nancy wished she had him there to help.

"I'm going to need your wig, Bess," Nancy said.

Bess clutched the dark Lynxette wig on her head. "My wig? Why?"

"No time to explain." Nancy turned to Ms. Long. "May I also borrow a pair of sunglasses and the last Morrell jacket?" Nancy nodded toward the candy-apple red jacket displayed at the front of the store.

Ms. Long twirled a rack of sunglasses and picked out a pair with red cat's-eye frames. "The glasses, you can borrow if you promise to bring them back. But the jacket is out of the question. I've been saving that one for my sister."

Nancy was undaunted. "Ms. Long, it could mean the difference between my catching the thieves or not. And if we don't stop them today, the problem won't go away. It'll get worse. But if my plan works, I guarantee the thieves will be brought to justice and you'll get all your jackets back."

Ms. Long shook her head, then heaved a sigh. Finally she relented. "All right." She took the candy-apple red jacket off the mannequin. "But if this jacket is stolen, my sister's going to be upset and I am going to be *very* angry."

"Trust me," Nancy said. Then she took Ms. Long aside and told her to try to track down

Frank—*quietly*—and tell him to head down to Davidson's loading dock.

Five minutes later Nancy and Bess were in the employee lounge, almost ready to go. Nancy was wearing Bess's black wig and the red Morrell jacket. Ruby red lipstick and the pair of sunglasses completed her disguise. She was now "Heather Harrison," author of the note she'd left. Craig would never recognize her. At least she hoped he wouldn't.

"There's film in the camera, right?" Nancy asked Bess, double-checking. "Is it fast film in case the light is bad?"

"Yes, there's film. I bought George a roll to replace the one she shot of me. And, yes, it's fast." Bess was clutching George's bright yellow underwater camera in both hands. She was terribly nervous, and Nancy only hoped she didn't get cold feet.

"And you know how to work the camera?"

"Yes, Nancy. I told you! Now, what am I supposed to do?"

"Okay. Pay attention. I want you to go out to the loading dock behind Davidson's Department Store. There's a small green Dumpster right on the dock. Go there and hide behind it. I'm going to be meeting Craig Jordan there to buy stolen Morrell jackets. As soon as you see him showing me the stolen jackets, start snapping pictures like crazy. Okay?"

Bess acted terribly uncomfortable. "Are

these guys dangerous? Shouldn't you call security?"

"There's no time. I hope Ms. Long has the sense to alert Frank."

"And that he's not in the middle of that crowd up there, trying to keep the kids in order," Bess added.

"Right," Nancy said. "I'm afraid that if we wait, Craig will sell all the jackets he's got, and then he'll never be caught."

"Right," Bess agreed, though she still sounded nervous.

"Just stay out of sight, Bess, and everything will be fine. And keep that camera under wraps until you need it. That yellow color might attract attention."

Bess nodded, but Nancy wasn't sure her nervous friend was absorbing all this. It was getting late, though, so there was no time to go through it again.

"Okay, let's go out the back door, so we don't have to deal with that crowd."

Bess nodded like a zombie as Nancy waited for her to unlock the door with Ms. Long's key, but then just stood there with the key in her hand.

"Bess, the door."

"Right, right. The door. I've got it. I've got it." Bess unlocked the door and let them out into the rear corridor.

Nancy bit her bottom lip and crossed her fingers behind her back.

* * *

At five minutes after three "Heather Harrison" was waiting for Craig Jordan on the loading dock. A chill breeze was blowing, and Nancy had to zip up the Morrell jacket for warmth. She'd felt funny putting on the glitzy disguise, but now she was beginning to wonder if it was all for nothing. Where was Craig? Could Mr. Olsen have forgotten to give him the note?

"Pssst! Nancy!" Bess called in a stage whisper from behind the Dumpster, in the shadows of the loading dock. "Do you see him?"

"Ssshhh!" Nancy said out of the corner of her mouth. "Just stay down and be quiet."

Nancy rubbed her arms as she scanned the parking lot. There was a lot of activity out there, cars and people coming and going, but there was no sign of Craig.

Then suddenly she heard something behind her. The heavy metal door that led into Davidson's Department Store swung open. Out of the shadows stepped two figures—Craig and Jake. Craig was wearing jeans, a black turtleneck, and black cowboy boots that looked brand-new.

Nancy gulped. She hadn't counted on Craig bringing his accomplice with him. Jake was carrying two big, overstuffed, brown plastic garbage bags over his shoulder. Nancy tried not to stare at the blue anchor tattoo on his hand until she remembered that she was wearing dark glasses and her eyes couldn't be seen.

"Heather?" Craig asked as he approached. "Heather Harrison?"

"Yes. Craig?"

Craig didn't answer. Jake stayed in the shadows. "I've got what you want," Craig said ominously.

"Great," Nancy said gleefully, trying to stay in character. "Let's see."

"Over here," Jake said gruffly. He set down the bag and opened it so she could look inside.

"How many do you have?" she asked.

"Two dozen," Craig said. "The ones in that bag all have the Lynxette patch on the back. It's a complete set, except for one."

"Cool," Nancy said. "So let's see one."

"Uh-uh," Jake said, shaking his head. "First let's see some cash."

Nancy hunched her shoulders. "That's not how *I* do business. First I see the merchandise, then we talk money." In fact, Nancy had no more than twenty dollars on her. She was going to have to bluff her way out of showing them money if it came to that.

Jake seemed reluctant, but he finally gave in, opening up the bag again. "Show her one," he said to Craig.

Craig pulled out the top jacket, a silver one, and held it up for Nancy to inspect. Nancy's pulse was racing. She hoped Bess was getting pictures of this.

"I want to see a few more," Nancy said.

Craig and Jake exchanged frowns, but they

did what she asked, pulling out a purple jacket, a gold one, and a lime green one. Nancy took her time inspecting each one, making Craig and Jake hold them up for her. She could feel the sweat dripping down the small of her back. Bess had better be getting some great shots, she thought.

"Can I see a few more?" she asked.

"Hey, what is this, a fashion show?" Craig balked. "They're all the same, just different colors."

Nancy stood right up to him. "I want to make sure I'm getting what I pay for. Is there a problem with that?"

"It will be if you don't show us some cash pretty soon," Craig snarled.

"That's right, sweetheart," Jake chimed in. "Put up or shut up."

Nancy knew she had to stand tough. "Look, if you're going to be that way about it, I'll just—"

Suddenly a camera flash went off. Bess pressed the wrong button! Nancy realized in horror as a gasp went up from behind the Dumpster.

"Oh, no!" Bess cried.

Jake was instantly furious. "Why, you little—"

"A camera?" Craig screamed. "Get her!" He lunged for Bess.

"Run, Bess, run!" Nancy shouted. "Get Frank!"

Bess ran full tilt for the door that led back

into Davidson's, but Craig was right on her tail. Nancy followed after them.

"Hey, wait!" Jake shouted. He threw the heavy bags of jackets over his shoulder and ran after Nancy.

They raced through the linen department of Davidson's and out into the lower level of the mall. "Call security!" Nancy yelled to a bewildered salesclerk. With everyone upstairs waiting for Lynxette, the first level of the mall was practically deserted. This was bad news because Craig with his long legs was going to catch up to Bess in no time.

"Don't stop," Nancy yelled to her friend. "Keep going, Bess."

Nancy's glasses slipped off as she ran. She hoped she could catch up with Craig and somehow waylay him, so Bess could get away. "Keep going, Bess! Keep—! Whoa!"

A meaty hand suddenly grabbed her arm from behind and yanked her back. It held her like a vise. "Heather Harrison, huh?" Jake growled, yanking off her wig. "You're going to pay for this." He started to pull her toward the exit to the parking lot.

But Nancy wasn't going to let that happen. She dug her fingers into one of the bulky garbage bags and ripped a gaping hole in it. A satiny rainbow of jackets spilled out onto the floor. "Why, you little—"

"Help! Police! Help!" Nancy shouted. "Help!"

A security guard on the upper level leaned

over the railing and pointed down at Jake. "You! Freeze! Don't move!"

Jake panicked, caught between recovering the valuable jackets and saving himself. In that moment of indecision, he loosened his grip, and Nancy twisted free, dashing off to catch up with Craig and Bess.

"Hold on, Bess. I'm coming!"

But up ahead Craig had already caught up with Bess at the edge of the big fountain in the central court. He roughly snatched the camera out of Bess's hand and sneered in her face.

"You think you're so smart?" he said. "All I have to do is open this camera and expose the film, and then you and your friend Nancy Drew will have nothing on me. Nothing!"

"Wrong, Craig." Nancy ran up behind him and snatched the camera back, quickly wrapping the long strap around her wrist, determined not to give it up.

"Give me that," Craig demanded as he grabbed at the camera. But Nancy was quicker than he was and dodged out of his reach.

"Give it to me!" he barked, but this time he grabbed her by the throat and pushed her back.

Nancy tried to keep the camera from him, but he wrestled it out of her hand. The strap was still wrapped securely around her wrist, though. It hurt when he pulled, but she wasn't going to let him have it.

"Give it to me!" he repeated. In a blind fury Craig shoved her hard, and she toppled backward over the edge of the fountain and into the water. The pool wasn't deep, two feet at the most, but the water was up to her neck because she was lying in it.

Craig kept pulling on the camera, trying to unravel the strap on her wrist, but Nancy was determined to keep it. That film was the only hard evidence she had against Craig and Jake, and she wasn't going to give it up.

Suddenly Craig jumped into the fountain, and grabbed her by the throat and dunked her under the water. He held her head down, pressing all his body weight on her. Nancy struggled, but he was too strong. Looking up, she could see his cold blue eyes. He was a horrible watery blur bent on drowning her.

She tried everything she could think of to break free, but it was no use. Water started to seep into her nostrils. Panic filled her chest as she started to choke. She needed air! Fast!

Chapter Sixteen

WITH HER LAST OUNCE of strength, Nancy pulled her knees up to her chest and mule-kicked Craig in the stomach. It was enough to get him off her, and she quickly sat up, coughing and gasping for breath. Craig was sitting in the water, stunned by her unexpected counterattack.

Nancy got to her feet, still coughing, but ready to take on Craig again if she had to.

Craig was glaring at her as he stood up and started wading toward her. "You're going to be so sorry you ever messed with me—"

"Don't even think about it, Craig." Standing at the edge of the pool, ready to jump in, was Frank Wexler. He was holding a nightstick, and he was ready to use it.

Craig's mouth hung open. Immediately he backed away from Nancy.

"Freeze!" A uniformed officer held a gun on him from the other side of the fountain, preventing his escape.

George was standing behind the officer. "Thank goodness I went back to Wicked," she called to Nancy. "Ms. Long told me to find Frank and get the police."

Nearby, two other officers were holding a very unhappy Jake by the elbows. He was in handcuffs.

"Come out of the fountain, son," the officer holding the gun ordered. As soon as Craig stepped out, he was handcuffed.

Frank rushed into the water to help Nancy. "Are you all right, Nancy? Are you hurt?"

Nancy was touched by his concern. "I'm fine," she said. "Just wet. Here. You better hang on to this." She handed him the camera, thankful that it was waterproof.

"That's him," Jake shouted, jerking his chin at Craig. "It was all his idea to steal the Morrell jackets. He asked me to help him, but I didn't want any part of it. Believe me, officers. I'm telling you the truth."

"What?" Craig said, stunned and angry. "You're in this with me—half and half—remember, *partner?* You've got people in malls all over the state stealing Morrell jackets."

Jake tried to act innocent. "Now, officers, why would I do that? It doesn't make sense. I have a very good job working for Lynxette. I don't need the cash. But *he* does. Everybody knows his rich old man won't give him any spending money. That's why he has to work as a maintenance man here. Rich boy here's the one with the motive."

Craig struggled to break free of his bonds. "He's a liar! We ran into each other in the food court about six months back when he came to promote Lynxette's video. I was complaining about needing cash. He came up with the idea of working together to set up the jacket craze. I had the know-how with security—he had an in with Morrell because of Lynxette. He could keep track of shipments and stuff."

Jake scoffed. "Why would I do that?" he blustered.

"You were afraid you'd lose your job with Lynxette if her record sales didn't pick up," Craig said. "You told me that yourself, Jake."

"That's not true!" Jake yelled. "Lynxette and I are solid. We—"

"*Used* to be solid, Jake." All eyes turned toward a very familiar voice coming from the edge of the small crowd that had gathered around the fountain. It was Lynxette. Her deep green eyes and dark pageboy hairstyle were unmistakable.

Bess inhaled sharply. Her eyes grew huge. She looked as if she was going to faint.

Lynxette had arrived with a police escort. "I heard all about the bags of Morrell jackets they caught you with, Jake. You're fired."

"But, Lynxette, sweetie," Jake pleaded. "I only did it for you."

"Maybe so, but it was a very bad idea. A

crime is a crime, and I don't condone crime. You know that."

"But, Lynxette—"

"But nothing. You're fired."

"But—"

"Sorry," she said, turning on her high heels, "but I've got a video to film." Her pageboy swished as she headed for the escalator, her bodyguards swarming around her.

Lesley Richards muscled her way to the front just as the officer who'd arrested Craig was about to take him away. "Craig! Craig! What's happening?"

But Craig refused to look her in the eye.

"Do you know him, young lady?" the officer asked sternly.

"Yes, he's my boyfriend—"

Craig cut her off. "Used to be her boyfriend." He lowered his voice and added with a note of pleading, "She had nothing to do with this, Officer. She's innocent. Believe me."

The man frowned. "Let's go, young man. You can call your parents from the station." He took Craig by the arm and led him toward the exit.

Lesley looked as if her whole world had just come crashing down on her. Nancy went to her and put her arm around her. Lesley buried her face in Nancy's shoulder.

"You were right about him, Nancy," Lesley said softly. "He was obsessed with money and buying things. He always talked about it, said he was going to show his father that he didn't need his money, that he'd get everything he ever wanted despite his father's old-fashioned ideas. I should have known Craig was up to something. I guess I just didn't want to see the truth."

"It's okay," Nancy consoled her. "It's not your fault."

"Nancy! Nancy Drew!" A strident voice carried over the heads of the crowd as Ms. Long fought her way to the front.

Suddenly Nancy realized that the Morrell jacket she was wearing was soaking wet, and it was the one Ms. Long had been saving for her sister. Nancy caught Bess's eye. Bess winced. They read each other's minds, both expecting the worst.

"Nancy!" Ms. Long said crisply.

Nancy looked down at the sopping jacket. "I'm sorry about the jacket, Ms. Long. I promise to—"

"For goodness sake, don't worry about the jacket," Ms. Long crowed, throwing her arms around Nancy. "You did it! You caught the thieves and recovered the new shipment. Thank you, Nancy, thank you."

Nancy was stunned. Bess's mouth was hanging open. Even George on the other side of the fountain looked shocked.

"Now, Bess," Ms. Long said crisply, "I suggest you get moving if you intend to be in that video. The other girls are waiting for you."

"But . . . but . . . Who's minding the store?"

"Don't worry. One of the clerks from Bookworms volunteered to hold the fort. Now hurry up. You have to change. The girls left another wig for you on top of your locker."

Ms. Long then turned back to Nancy and looked her up and down, frowning. "You're going to catch pneumonia if you don't get out of those clothes. Come with me." Ms. Long took Nancy by the arm and led her to the escalator.

Thirty minutes later Nancy emerged from Wicked in a complete new outfit, courtesy of Ms. Long. She was wearing a gold-embroidered black vest over an ivory silk blouse, a pair of black designer jeans, and the chili-pepper red cowboy boots that she'd had her eye on.

Up on the runway outside the store, Lynxette was singing her new single called "Am I the One?" while dozens of Lynxette look-alikes in dark pageboy wigs and Morrell jackets danced around her. It took Nancy only a moment to find Bess in the chorus line. Nancy waved, and Bess grinned back as she danced. She seemed to be nodding toward something in the crowd.

Nancy followed her friend's gaze and spotted Dan Schaffer in the crowd with his eyes glued to Bess. Standing next to him were George and Darryl, formerly Mr. X. He had his arm around her shoulder, and they were swaying to the music, obviously having a fantastic time. Nancy was so intent in watching her friends, she didn't notice Frank walk up behind her.

"Good work, Nancy Drew," his baritone voice whispered in her ear. She turned around and found herself inches from his chest. "Hey," he said, "don't we have a rain check for something?"

Nancy nodded. "For something." She began to grin.

Frank nodded his head toward the escalator. "Lynxette is great—but I bet the arcade is empty."

Nancy arched her eyebrows and shouldered her bag. "I'm game," Nancy replied.

Frank smiled at the challenge in her eyes and led her through the crowd. "There's a new Maze Maniac."

"Sounds great to me," Nancy said. She gave a quick look over her shoulder. Bess and George wouldn't even miss her.

Even though Nancy was still sore and a little bruised from her ordeal with Craig, she found herself beaming. She was with Frank and her friends were having the time of their lives. Best of all, the shoplifter of the River Heights Mall was permanently out of business.

Nancy's next case:

Bess has landed a small part in a promising new Chicago play, and she's seeing stars for the hot young featured actor, Jordan McCabe. Nancy, however, sees only trouble. The play is a mystery, the theme is murder, and it soon becomes apparent that Nancy and Bess may both have starring roles in a deadly real-life drama. A mysterious fire backstage, a prop gun loaded with real bullets, and an anonymous threat on Bess's life put Nancy on notice that danger is waiting in the wings. Nancy's investigation turns up a whole cast of suspects . . . one of whom is determined to turn the final act into a major tragedy . . . in *Rehearsing for Romance,* Case #114 in The Nancy Drew Files™.